WILDERNESS

MIDNIGHT SUN 1

LYNN BURKE

WILDERNESS

I'm an adrenaline junkie.

I get off on tempting fate—until the day I make a reckless misstep that claims three lives.

The Alaskan bush offers the perfect opportunity to overcome survivor's guilt and find peace: Live off grid in seclusion where a mistake only threatens one life—my own.

My only tie to humanity is a feisty bush pilot who hates everything I am. Even though the connection between us blazes like a forest fire, she's determined to keep her distance.

The backcountry has other plans, however, and I end up with her life in my hands.

Unknown to me, there's a tenacious huntsman on her tracks, shadowing her every move, and one wrong choice leaves her vulnerable.

He takes what's mine.

A wild beast rises inside me, and the hunter becomes the prey. I will level mountains, fight the untamed wilderness, to save her—even if I leave a path of carnage behind me.

1

BROCK

The Alaskan wilderness stretched around me as far as I could see, mountains cutting the sky shut on all sides of the horizon, offering what I sought—that fucking high, that rush of *life* coming at me, screaming—daring—me to grab hold and ride the storm. Rugged and untamed, the land called to me in a way I hadn't experienced in far too long.

I'd left the East Coast in search of solitude away from the public eye and the judgmental stares of those who recognized my face from being plastered over the news two years earlier. Need to prove myself kept me driving away from Fairbanks, a lone cabin, off-grid and out in the woods, my final destination.

Mom had asked while hugging me goodbye if I would ever return to Boston. I doubted it.

Unless a grizzly decided I would make a tasty snack, I planned on growing gray-haired and hobble-y far from man —or woman. I'd seen a half-dozen of the huge, hairy fuckers in the past couple of days, and I'll admit to a bit of fear at the thought of being faced with one. Way bigger than my six feet if standing on its hind legs, way broader than my wide shoulders, one of those brown, bushy bears would take me down with one damn swipe of its massive paws.

Nightmares from my childhood contained snarling grizzlies and still shivered my skin—but bring on the snow, ice, and howling wind. Bring on the negative temperatures and snug log cabin smelling of wood smoke and roasting wild game.

I'd outfitted myself with the best money could buy, and the supplies packed underneath the fiberglass cap of my truck spoke truth of that fact.

The old man's cabin I'd bought off his son six months earlier had come fully furnished, and I'd bought the property as-is without having seen more than online pictures. No electricity. No running water. No sewage. No heat other than what I would supply by hand with my chainsaw and axe.

I'd climbed the highest mountains. Gone spelunking in the deepest caves. Thrown myself out of planes with nothing more than a sheet of nylon to keep me from face-splatting on the earth. Deep sea diving had placed me in shark territory. Anything that offered an adrenaline rush drew me in like a red, waving flag to a bull hell-bent on defeating its opponent.

One mistake, one second of losing focus, had made me responsible for three deaths—and had left me sitting with therapist after therapist trying to deal with survivor's guilt. It was time to move the fuck on.

Start my next adventure.

My lips twitched into a grin as I passed a worn-down sign announcing the next shit town—if it could even be called such. No stop lights, no sprawling shopping center. One bar and one motel-like place in desperate need of a coat of paint flanked the road with a few other dilapidated buildings farther up the two-lane highway.

I pulled into the motel's gravel parking lot, having already made reservations for the night.

In the morning, I would head an hour up the road to the airstrip of Midnight Sun Charter and fly out into the wilderness where I would be reborn. Having come highly recommended by a friend of a friend of a friend, we'd discussed details by email, confirming for a morning flight including all my supplies.

I could have gone with the bigger charter service out of Fairbanks, but I'd always been a supporter of the local businesses, the small fish in the pond who tended to scurry and be ever watchful in order to fill its belly. You wouldn't get laziness from those boys—something I couldn't stand in myself or others. Deep in the wilds, there wouldn't be time for lackadaisical attitudes. If I didn't work, I didn't eat. Didn't enjoy heat. Didn't get to rest comfortably.

Yearning to start the challenge ahead of me pumped adrenaline through my system, and I knew attempting sleep before nine would be an absolute joke.

A turn of the key shut my truck down, and I drank in the silence I'd never had issue with. While my brother needed the chatter and phones in our family's office building back in downtown Boston, I hadn't been able to stand the fucking place with its constant noise. As the oldest, he would be taking over when Dad decided to retire. But he'd be running the business alone—without me or his fiancé whose death I'd been responsible for. Not that he'd wanted me within fifty yards of him since.

Lips in a grim line, I hopped out of my truck into the cool evening, giving my stiff, aching leg a few seconds to relax. Determined to focus on the present rather than the past like my therapists suggested, I filled my lungs with clean air scented with soil and pine.

Country music played from somewhere behind me, and I turned, taking note of the propped open doorway of the pub across the street. With it being the only food joint around from what I could tell, I planned on heading there once settled. A car door slammed, and a horn honked somewhere close by, drawing my gaze around an area too settled for my taste. Less than a dozen people meandered in the vicinity, but I drew each and every ones' stares.

Stranger in town, just passing through—at least that's what I told anyone curious enough to ask. And there'd been plenty of nosy fuckers every place I'd stopped on my trek across the continent.

Stretching out my neck, I started off toward the door stating *Office* in faded white lettering, my bum leg loosening with each step. The old woman manning the desk handed over a key in exchange for cash—no signature, no credit card on file. No questions either, surprisingly. No Wi-Fi, something I would gladly live without.

Needing to make a few calls before hiding myself away, I let myself into my room and dropped my overnight bag onto the double bed. Worn out bedspread, saggy mattress in the middle, and limp pillows didn't promise a good night's sleep, but I hadn't slept more than four hours straight in two years, anyway. Even with help from meds, I couldn't find rest. Night after night, my mind went to that day that had changed the course of my life.

Dropping onto the bed, I grimaced at the squeaking box spring, and powered my satellite phone to life. I'd paid a pretty penny for the damn thing only because my mom insisted I have some means of communication.

I called Mom first, letting her know I'd made it safely to Alaska, offering my final goodbyes to her and Dad once she put me on speaker phone so he could hear. She promised to call me on my birthday, at Thanksgiving, and Christmas. She shed a few tears, but my eyes remained dry as the dust in the Sahara I'd gotten my fill of. While I loved my family, things hadn't been the same since I'd killed the love of my brother's life.

I missed my buddies more than my blood. If shit got too real out there in no-man's land, they'd be the first I would reach out to. I'd set up a 4-man text group prior to leaving the Boston area, and we'd been in touch throughout my cross-country trek. Adam seemed the most disapproving with the route I'd decided to take with my life, but having a couple of kids, I thought, would change a man's mind on living a selfish life.

I didn't want kids. No fucking thank you.

Rian and his woman were still trying, last I'd heard.

Both Jordan and Garret also had rug rats—one each.

Once their marriages had turned into families, they'd stopped congregating at Adam's estate up in New Hampshire to play in the old church he'd outfitted into a BDSM paradise. Not that I'd ever partaken in their lifestyle. Knew all about it, though. Knew how all three men met their submissive wives, went to their weddings, and watched them tie knots with their claimed soul mates.

Personally, I didn't think such a thing existed. I'd had my fair share of women and not a single one had tempted me into offering a chance at forever. I had too much living to do, and since the accident, I knew I never wanted to be responsible for another soul ever again.

My final night in society, I texted the group.

Of course, Jordan's reply came through first. **Any pussy to be had?**

Me: **Haven't gone looking.**

Jordan: **Get your ass in gear, man. You're going to be shut up with nothing but your goddamn fist.**

Adam: **If that isn't deterrent enough…**

I ignored Adam's invite to argue. Been there, done that, and nothing would change my mind.

Rian: **Best of luck out there, buddy**

Jordan's, **I hope you find peace, my friend**, came through at the same time.

Feeling as though I'd already started to, I found my lips twitching again. **I will**, I texted back.

Garrett: **May your cupboards be full, and may you find a cute little Eskimo woman to warm your lumpy mattress in that ramshackled shit box you spent good money on.**

Jordan: **He likes blondes, asshole.**

Rian: **Didn't you date a redhead once?**

Chuckling, I shot back a thumbs up. Let the fuckers take it however the hell they wanted. I did spend too much for my wilderness getaway like Garrett had said, but the cost hadn't dented my bank account or investments.

Adam: **I give him three months.**

Me: **Before?** A frown dented my brow. Fucker hadn't been anything but a Debbie Downer since I'd told them I was going off-grid.

Adam: **You're on the hunt for pussy. Might want to consider taking a goat along. Fresh milk and all that.**

I barked a laugh. **Go fuck yourself.**

Adam: **A hole is a hole is a hole…**

Garrett: **Sick fuck. Leave the man alone.**

Rian: **I gotta side with Adam on this one.**

Jordan steered the conversation, telling me to take care of myself and call at any time, for any reason. The other three chimed in with the same.

A pang of something I couldn't name ached through my

chest, and I rubbed over my pecs before replying. Water stains ran across the motel room's ceiling, its lone light bulb in the middle of the room barely illuminating the chair and small table in the far corner. Nothing like the five-star hotels I'd stayed in across the world.

I wouldn't want to be any place else, though.

Deciding on one last text before powering my phone down, I took my time typing out the words to my best friends —just in case they were my last. Fuck knew what the morning would bring. My first flight since the day that Old Betsy went down...

Throat swelling, I read over my text.

Thank you all for your friendship, especially over the last couple of years. I appreciate your loyalty even when half of my family turned their backs on me. I'm not saying goodbye for good, but if this is my last adventure in life, know that I'll be thinking of you when my life flashes before my eyes. Take care of yourselves, love the hell out of your wives, and kiss all those cute brats for me. Rian, best of luck in knocking up your sexy little Luna. I'll see you on the other side.

Lips pressed in a tight line, I hit send and turned off my phone.

Time for one last burger, fries, and a couple of beers. Hopefully, the shit hole across the road could make my last night around humans a good one.

2

JESSIE

Talk about a shitty day from hell. First, having to drive into Fairbanks to meet with my CPA to get my taxes filed—late as usual—and having to hear the know-it-all man spew shit about a woman having no place being a bush pilot.

Well fuck him and the pencils that had to endure his too-smooth-palm touch.

Then running into *him*, the asshole who didn't understand the meaning of the word "no", the bastard who'd stolen my father's charter business when he'd hit troubled waters. Spoiled rich asshole who thought he owned the world, or that he could buy what he didn't already lord over.

Getting groceries for the next couple of months was usually a chore I enjoyed, loading up a couple of carts with bulk supplies, but that fucking ass just happened to appear at the end of the first aisle, ruining my mood I'd managed to pull out of the gutter after leaving my CPA.

I pretended I didn't see him, but every inch of my body became aware of his presence as he neared.

His blue eyes twinkled in a way that most women would find attractive, his mousy brown hair with hints of gray tumbling in curls over his forehead in a seemingly innocent air, but something in his gaze hinted at an unhinged mind. Beyond spoiled, something a bit more … something not quite right.

"Hey, Jessie." He nudged against my shoulder like we were long lost pals or some such shit even though he had a good fifteen years on me.

I showed him my teeth with an audible snarl and kept walking, trying to shake off the creepy vibes he'd dumped over my head from a simple, totally intentional, bump of his arm against me.

Cort Endsley freaked me the fuck out.

Not for the first time, I ignored his sense of entitlement when it came to women. I loved that I couldn't be bought, that I could stand on my own two feet—he hated it.

I thought I lost him when he didn't show up in the next two aisles. My shoulders relaxed, and I focused on the long as hell list in my hand.

"It doesn't have to be this way," he whispered against my ear, and I squeaked, jumping damn near a foot in the air.

"The fuck!" I whispered harshly and spun, ready to clock him in the damn nose, but too many people stood close by. While I might not be able to obtain a restraining order due to his cousin being the sheriff, he had the money and status to drag my name through the shitter and ruin my family's business that I'd struggled to rebuild the previous five years.

"Fuck off, Cort," I muttered, list crumpled in my fist as I shoved the cart forward.

"I'm tired of waiting, Jessie," he called after me.

"Then find someone else to bother," I shot over my shoulder, giving him my best resting bitch face.

"But you're the prettiest thing I've seen. Your fire draws me in like a moth to the flame, baby."

I rolled my eyes, ignoring the titters of two grandmotherly types I paused beside.

"You're sunshine and moonlight," Cort continued, drawing an, "Aw" from both women. "I dream about you barefoot and pregnant in my kitchen every night."

I snorted. The fucker probably hated that my reputation as a pilot, a mere woman, rivaled his own. In his mind, I expected, a woman had no business being anywhere but pregnant and in the kitchen.

"He only wants to get his dick wet," I told the old women, bending to grab a case of diced tomatoes.

One old lady gasped. The other snickered and dragged her friend away as I hoisted the flat of cans into my cart.

"Jessie."

I ignored Cort, grabbing up a case of canned corn a few feet farther down the aisle. The old ladies disappeared around the corner, and we stood alone.

Fuck.

The hairs rose on my arms, and my heart kicked into high gear in the worst way possible.

"I always get what I want." The heat of him pressed close —but didn't touch—and still, a shiver slid down my spine, curdling the frothy cappuccino in my stomach I'd splurged on in attempts to forget my earlier meeting.

"Not this time, you don't," I reminded him, my voice shaking as I hurried up the aisle.

The asshole grabbed my arm and spun me, his fingers digging into my flesh through the light flannel I wore. "Give me what I want, and you can have your daddy's precious plane back," he spit.

I jerked from his hold, hissing a few curses under my breath. My daddy's plane that I longed to own but couldn't afford—and I refused to pay for it with anything but cash.

Cort wasn't having it. "You fucking touch me again, you sick prick, and I'll get that restraining order."

"You can try." He grinned, contrary to the harsh hold on my arm, flashing pearly whites I wanted to knock back into his throat. Maybe he would choke to death…

"Fucking crooked ass cops." I shoved my cart forward, yanking free of his grasp.

"I'm tired of this cat and mouse game," Cort said, sticking to my backside, his voice losing all trace of jollity. "Don't give me what I want, and I'll destroy you, Jessie Blacke. Your business. Your Daddy's precious name. *Your* reputation."

He'd said the same once before—I'd even gotten his damn voice recorded with those threats—but the cops in his back pocket didn't give a shit.

The smart fucker never approached me in private where I could retaliate without fear of retribution. All I needed was one time, one opportunity, to get him in close proximity where no witnesses would see me take revenge for ruining my family's name.

Temptation to give in to what he wanted for the sake of getting him alone warred with my sense of self-preservation. At five-foot-one, I had to crane my neck to meet his lascivious gaze with a hardened one of my own. He packed muscle while I barely managed to hold up a pair of jeans with my too-small, good for nothing, ass. At least I had tits aplenty, so I didn't look like a teenage boy from a distance.

Popping a bullet into his brain from afar was my best bet, but I couldn't even stomach shooting an animal to feed myself through the winter.

"No, no, and no. It'll always be no, Cort. Leave. Me. Alone." I bit out the words and spun, praying like hell he'd listen.

"You forget the funds at my disposal, Jessie."

Fucking asshole.

"You're going to regret that answer, one way or another," he called after me.

I ignored his threat and kept walking. Two aisles later, I breathed a sigh of relief while grabbing the last item on my list, and I managed to pay for my over-flowing cart full of groceries and get the hell out of town without running into the rich asshole again.

My shitty day got worse when I stopped to fill up my old truck's tank and checked my messages.

The supply shipment I had scheduled for the following week had cancelled.

"Goddamnitalltohell," I muttered and pressed my lips tight. I needed every penny to stay afloat. Losing one shipment wasn't so big a deal, but with it being a long-time customer who stated Cort had offered him a better rate…

I could only imagine what else my archrival and creepy stalker had told the man about me—all because I refused to fuck him.

Still cursing in my head, I topped off my tank and climbed back into my truck, the rusty door slamming from my over-zealous yanking. Windows down, I tore off toward home, scowling and ready to punch something. Someone. The state I found myself in, had Cort been close by, I'd have attempted to make him choke on his pearly whites.

I need a fucking drink.

Home lay a couple hours away—too far away. If I'd had the funds, I'd have stayed at a hotel in town with a bottle of Jameson to make love to all damn night long. My luck, Cort would somehow find me and force his way into my room. Wouldn't put it past the fucker. The energy rolling off him lay far beyond the creep factor, straight into rapist-city if I had to wager a guess. No amount of pleading or money would get me alone with him willingly.

I'd left him in Fairbanks, wishing I could leave behind the memory and oily feeling on my skin lingering from his hot whispers near my ear. Another shiver slid over me, and I cursed him to hell and back again.

A little shit town lay halfway between me and home, and I decided to stop in at The Watering Hole for some whiskey. Even better would be a good hard fuck. Hadn't had one of those in so damn long, I couldn't remember. Whoever the last had been, he didn't haunt my dreams with a big cock or talented tongue. Hell, no one I'd been with had rocked my world. Not even one had launched me into the stratosphere or sent me soaring into the clouds like my old '56 Beaver.

Best bush plane ever. My baby cost me every cent of my inheritance when my great aunt Silvia passed, and it'd been the best money I'd ever spent.

A few years older than Dad's Beaver, mine purred like a kitten and floated in the sky, every gust of wind like a lover's caress over her solid frame. She'd been updated with modern electronics, making my job an absolute joy.

My throat tightened as memories of Dad teaching me to fly slid through my mind. We'd spent hours together, had been tighter than anything. Two damn peas in a pod who looked alike, with Mom being our carrot. A perfect combination, the perfect family and home life.

That perfection had ended two days after my fourteenth birthday when they had scrounged up enough money to go out to dinner for their anniversary. Something had distracted Dad enough he'd turned the car sideways while on the open road, rolling it four times according to the police report. There'd been no witnesses, no evidence of what had made Dad lose control.

An excellent pilot, a driver with a clean record who didn't speed, Dad had always stayed alert. Didn't drink and drive. Didn't even have a cell phone to fiddle with while behind the wheel.

Years later, once I learned what had happened to Dad's planes and business due to a gambling debt of all things, I wondered over the "accidental" part of their deaths. Dad wasn't a stupid man, but once of age, my great aunt and Dad's CPA finally told me he'd been gambling for years and owed a very rich man—Cort Endsley—a hell of a lot of money. What was left of their estate upon their deaths didn't come close to covering that debt.

At least I hadn't been liable for the rest of it.

Cort got the family business, all my parents' assets, and our old home in the sticks to cover part of what had been owed him. I ended up an orphan and got nothing—until my great aunt died, leaving me her sole heir. With the monetary inheritance, I'd begun rebuilding my family business. With her twenty acres and old log cabin out in the sticks, I'd kept the home I'd known since fourteen.

Eyes hazing, I fought to focus on the road and tiny town growing in the distance ahead. No sense living in the past. I couldn't do a damn thing about it but trudge onward and make my DBA, Midnight Sun Charter, as successful as it had been when I'd been a kid.

If I could rebuild the business to where Dad had taken it before losing it all to Cort, I knew I could get back a piece of what I'd lost. Accomplishing that goal wouldn't bring my parents back, but at least a part of me would feel complete.

I had a twenty in my back pocket, enough for a couple shots of whiskey. Sitting in the bar and unloading on Dale, the old bartender, might help to ease the burden of my shit day. He had a good ear and had known Mom and Dad. He also knew about my stalker and how the cops wouldn't do jack shit to keep me safe. And even though he was partial to the three S's—shoot, shovel, and shut up—he didn't support my wanting to bury the asshole.

Slamming my driver door after hopping from my old Ford gave me a sense of satisfaction, and I strode into the bar with a rush of wind whipping my chin-length hair around my head. Tucking it back behind my ears, I focused on Dale behind the bar and the bottle of whiskey he grabbed upon seeing my scowling face.

3

BROCK

The bulk of patrons at The Watering Hole lounged at tables behind me, their voices a din atop the country music filtering through out of sight speakers. No TVs. No pool tables or dart boards. No hot women to tempt me into living my last night with humanity to its fullest.

Just as well. I wasn't in the mood to make small talk or get personal enough to weasel my way between a woman's thighs.

If the patrons of the shit bar knew what I'd done, I'd be ostracized just like I'd been back home. Staying private kept inner turmoil brought on by assholes away. I had enough of my own to deal with.

Best to keep to myself. Dale, the bartender and owner, had taken my one-worded answers to his prying questions as the hint I'd meant them to be and left me alone.

My love of adrenaline highs and survivalist camps never mind my month-long stint on the popular TV show, Seclusion, held my confidence at a cocky high as I considered the path ahead of me. My drive for life, to find a reason for my sad existence, had kept me barreling forward at an alarming rate all through my teens and twenties. Kept me walking the edge, climbing the mountains, flying to new heights, and leaping downward, spiraling with my arms wide open. Adrenaline junkie, my family had called me.

It's what brought on the end of too many lives.

Scowling and absently rubbing at my knee, I drank down the rest of my warm beer, ready to order something a bit stronger.

The bar's door opened, letting in a blast of cool spring air, and a petite woman strode in like a hurricane, stealing my thoughts and breath. Her hair hung on the shorter side, white-blonde and blunt cut at her raised, pointy chin. Glacial blue eyes hinted at her intent for entering. Gaze on Dale, she moved with purpose in worn-out hiking boots without sparing a quick glance around the bar, her lips in a thin line.

A whole lot of piss and vinegar wrapped up in one tiny package in tight jeans and a blue flannel that buttoned tight to her slight waist and spilled open around huge tits smooshed into a white tank top beneath.

My dick took interest in pussy for the first time in two years, and the second she rasped out, "You read my mind, Dale," I bit back a groan. Husky voice, low and sexy as fuck, fully woke my dick the hell up.

Dale nodded and served her a cheap whiskey without a word. She slapped a twenty on the bar with one hand while lifting the shot with her other.

"You okay, little girl?" the older bartender asked, his gray eyebrows furrowed.

"Will be."

"The asshole?"

"Yep." She downed the liquor like a pro, without a flinch, licking her lower lip when finished. "Another."

Dale poured, and I shifted on my seat, two stools away, my dick aching.

My movement caught her attention, and that blue-eyed gaze landed on me, snagging my breath again clear from my lungs again. Her slow, crooked smirk and swelling pupils did funny things to my insides, and I couldn't decide if I liked the foreign feeling or not.

"Hello, there, stranger," she purred and held my stare with a hungry one of her own while pointing at the stool beside me. "Seat taken?"

Shaking my head, I sat back as though comfortable as hell, hands on my thighs, beer forgotten, while the nerve endings in my body came alive with a sexual adrenaline high I'd used to chase after every damn chance I'd gotten—and hadn't felt in what seemed like forever.

The sexy vixen slid onto the seat beside me and glanced at the bottle on the bar in front of me. "Can I buy you a drink?"

"Sure."

"Dale," she said without looking at him, her knee starting to bounce with pent-up energy or nervousness. "New to town?" Her voice didn't betray the latter. The little vixen was pure confidence, and if I had to guess, just as driven and impatient as me.

"Just passing through."

Dale poured me a shot in my periphery.

"Where ya headed?" she asked, grabbing up her shot glass.

I did the same. "Up the road a bit."

Her lips twitched with a hint of her crooked smile over my vague answer, and we drank together, our gazes locked, energy crackling the air between us. The pulse in her neck thrummed in time with mine, and my dick jerked inside my pants at the thought of getting my teeth on the hard nipples poking against both the tank top and flannel.

It'd been one hell of a long time since I'd felt instant lust for a woman, and the fact she felt it, too, decided my mind for the rest of the evening. Small talk would come easy, I didn't doubt, since there wouldn't be a need to weasel between her thighs. The vixen was ripe for the plucking, all but begging for my dick with her eyes. I expected I wouldn't even have to spill a single piece of shit of my past to end up where I felt sure we both wanted me to be.

"I had one shitty day," she said before I could officially hit on her, setting her glass back on the bar.

Dale poured without her asking, as though she was one of his loyal patrons and he knew when she needed her drink. I didn't wave off his offer to refill mine while considering the woman's statement.

"The rest is on me," I murmured to Dale.

"Why, thank you, handsome," the vixen purred again, forcing me to bite back another groan.

I wanted those damn tight jeans off her legs, and if being an ear for her to unload about said shitty day got me between her thighs, I wouldn't mind listening to her husky voice. Strangely, I actually wanted to know what had put the cold glint in her eyes, what prompted her to down cheap whiskey like water, and kept her knee hopping a few inches from mine.

That fact made me feel less like an asshole.

"I'm a good listener," I said, knowing I spoke truth. Being a personal pilot for a handful of bastards even richer than myself back in the Boston area had been the same as acting like the local bartender. A few had become friends, the only people besides Mom who would miss me.

The woman glanced down over my attire again, from the

Ray-Bans sitting atop my head, down over the Arc'teryx long-sleeved t-shirt hugging my pecs, the same brand hiking pants I hadn't skimped on, and the EverStep hiking boots I had propped on the stool's rails.

"Rich boy from Boston," she murmured, her brow furrowing.

Guess my attire and accent gave me away. Not bothering to argue, I grinned.

She returned to her drink and tipped her head back to swallow the whiskey down, drawing my focus to the smooth white skin of her neck.

So, she didn't like men with money—that much was obvious, but mind set on having her, I wasn't going to give up without a fight.

"So, are you going to tell me what lit that craving for whiskey in your gut?" I toyed with my shot glass while she considered her empty one, her lips returning to that line.

I sipped, waiting for her to spill.

Pointed chin lifting again, she turned toward me as though she'd made up her mind as well, that cold glint returning to her eyes even though her lust for my dick didn't dissipate in the least. She looked down her nose at me the best she could from her shorter perch, as though disgusted by my obvious money.

"A rich asshole I know who thinks he can take what he wants, when he wants, and doesn't seem to understand what no means," she snipped.

My spine went rigid with sudden need to protect a woman I didn't know from Adam, even though she definitely judged me as someone similar. It was that same instinct of taking on responsibility I never wanted to experience ever again.

It should have been me.

"Not all rich men are pricks," I decided to go with rather

than dwell on what had prompted my flight from society. I'd had enough of that shit for the day.

"Hmm." She waved Dale off when he offered another. "Perhaps not."

I leaned in close to catch a whiff of sweet vanilla that rushed drool to my mouth. "So, tell me who this bastard is so I can go kick his ass."

She let out an abrupt laugh, the bell-like tone higher than I'd have thought with how low her voice escaped her pouty lips. A sparkle softened her eyes to more a greenish-blue than frigid, her smile fixed in place. "Acting all tough and protective won't get you in my pants, Mr. Rich Boy."

My lips twitched along with my dick while I stared at the plump bit of flesh her tongue flicked out to moisten. "What will, Ms. Vixen?"

She glanced down over my relaxed form again. "Me."

A controlling little snit—the need to conquer lit inside me, and I grinned. "Your way or the highway, huh?"

"Damn right."

I'd never had a woman do what she'd done to my insides within five minutes. While I never backed down from a challenge, something tingled at the base of my skull, that sixth sense I often ignored whenever danger rose in the way of my intended destination.

Dale moved off, leaving us alone, so I leaned in closer, crowding her personal space. Her lips parted, but not an ounce of fear or reservation shaded her expressive eyes.

"So, how do you like it, Ms. Vixen?" I murmured, staring at her lips. "Hard and fast against a wall? Sprawled out on a bed in offering to a starving man? Bent over a chair? In the back of a truck beneath the stars?"

Her smirk damn near killed me. "Depends on the man."

I raised an eyebrow and waited, close enough she could have eased the tingle in my lips if she wanted.

"What about a rich, little asshole from Boston who's just passing through?" I pushed when she continued to hold my stare without a goddamn word.

She glanced at my crotch as I shifted to ease the ache in my balls. "Not so little."

"Damn right," I repeated her words and eased back in my chair with a grin, letting her eyes get their fill of the hard length straining against my pants.

"No strings attached." She tore her focus off my dick, her eyes more green than blue with arousal.

"Not a one."

"Don't need a name, either," she said.

"Fine by me, Ms. Vixen."

She glanced at my groin again and licked her lower lip. "Tempting, Mr. Rich Boy."

Tempting. I wanted to snort. The woman had no idea what kind of siren vibes radiated off her body and from her eyes. Pulled me in to the point every muscle in me vibrated with energy, and my knee took up jumping like hers continued to do.

Or maybe she did know her effect on men and liked to tease and play hard to get. Well, fuck that. I only had the one night—strings or no fucking strings—and I wanted a taste of that pale skin hiding beneath her tank top.

"Want to take a walk across the street?" I tossed out, praying like fuck she wanted in my pants as much as I did hers.

"Staying at the Ritz?"

The Ritz. I let out a small chuckle. "Cute nickname."

"Fitting." Her focus slipped to the bulge in my pants. "Clean?"

I caught her meaning by the calculating glint in her eye. Nothing better than a woman hell-bent on getting what she wants. "As a whistle."

"Safe, too?" Her husky voice lowered, her knee stilling. "Or do I need to hold a knife to your throat while fucking you?"

Goddamn, that mouth.

I had to adjust myself so I could lean forward again and fill my lungs with her sweet scent. "Woman, you can ride my dick any way you like. Forward, backward, bump or grind— won't hear any complaints from me."

"Let's go."

We'll, shit. I nearly chuckled. Damn easiest pick up in my entire life.

Ms. Vixen slid off her stool and strode toward the exit as determined as she'd entered.

I hopped up, dug a hundred-dollar bill from my pocket, and placed my shot glass atop it. Dale could keep the change.

Lovely swaying hips disappearing out the bar's door tore all my own shit from my head, and I had every intention of drowning beneath the hurricane of Ms. Vixen before burying myself in the vast wilderness of the north.

Getting used to Alaska's spring daylight hours would take time, but I wasn't about to complain over having a perfectly clear view of her backside while following her across the street at eight at night. Thick and juicy enough to bite, her thighs sent a shot of lust straight to my balls, seizing them up tight against my groin.

I groaned but lengthened my stride to walk alongside her since she didn't know which room was mine. Feeling like a giant came easy since my six foot plus height stood me a head and then some above her. A little pixie with the pointy chin to match…

"How tall are you?" I asked.

She snorted and glanced up at me, not breaking her pace as we crossed the street. "Five-one. Why?"

"You pack a whole lot of fire in one little package."

That greenish tint softened her eyes. "You have no idea."

I didn't really—but found myself wanting to.

She's just pussy for the night, not a hot as fuck woman to get caught up in.

I recognized the need to keep my heart locked up tight so I wouldn't leave it behind come morning, but I sure as fuck would take my memories of our time together into the solitude waiting for me.

4

___

JESSIE

R ich or not, the newest stranger in town was one fine specimen of a man and his bulge looked perfect for the hard fuck I desperately needed to get my mind off my shitty day. While his obvious money would usually keep me from giving him a second glance, his dark as espresso eyes and full lips made my knee bounce like mad.

"Down at the end." My conquest of the night angled toward our right through the motel's parking lot, and I followed, hurrying to keep stride with his long legs even though he limped slightly, my ability to focus in real time finally hindered by all the shots I'd done. I'd definitely had one too many.

He seemed in a rush, but with a hate fuck ahead of me, I didn't expect I'd get off too quickly. Perhaps I would ride his dick with a knife to his throat to make sure I got to enjoy myself before he busted a nut and filled me full of his cum.

A shiver licked over my spine at the thought of what he packed between his thighs. Fuck knew he hadn't bothered hiding what I did to him—and that turned me the hell on.

Already swollen and damp, my pussy couldn't wait to suck him in balls deep.

"I haven't been with anyone in two years."

My eyebrows shot up at his confession as he pulled out his room key from his back pocket and stopped in front of room three. "Why the fuck not?"

"Not interested." He'd hesitated to answer, his tone hinting at a juicy story, but he was only passing through, and I didn't allow anyone inside my head or heart.

"Two years is a long time. You gonna blow early and leaving me hanging?" I asked rather than dig with my usual nosiness as I followed him into his room.

"I'll wear your ass out long before I feel your pussy wrapped around my dick."

Said pussy spasmed. *Fuck, the confidence in his rumbling tone…*

He closed us in and grasped my arm, yanking me close before I could move deeper into the room.

Fire raced up my arm, but my back met the door with a thud.

Hungry lips laid claim, and my body came alive with a rush so damn toxic, I gasped, giving him an opening to devour my mouth. Whiskey and hops, hard muscle and male musk—downright delicious. Addictive. Too bad he wouldn't be around for me to sample in the future.

Pulling him closer trapped me in, and I didn't give a fuck in that moment if he meant me ill will or not. All thought but *take* swept me away on a lustful wind, one I couldn't withstand. I'd had drunken fucks before, so I couldn't blame the whiskey for my need for the stranger's dick.

He yanked at my jeans, mouth still plundering, and I did the same to him, my damn hands trembling while fighting with the clasp on his pants.

My stomach sucked in as he shoved his hand down the front of my gaping jeans, and I gasped again as his fingers slid down through my slickened, lower lips.

A deep groan rumbled against my mouth. "Fuck, little vixen—so damn wet."

"Mmm," I agreed, nipped his lip, and finally got access to his cock. Commando. Nothing in the way of warm, steel-like flesh and my palm.

Holy hell, he's hung.

He slid two fingers deep inside me at the same time I squeezed his girth, and a rush of arousal swept over me. Need for his cock set my sights on having it.

I bit down on his lip and squeezed the hell out of him, ripping a strangled grunt from his chest. "On the bed, rich boy."

He shoved his pants to his ankles, not bothering to take off his boots, and sat on the bed's edge, thighs spread, hand slowly jacking his length, and his focus on my heaving chest. "Let me see those tits, vixen."

Sauntering closer, I slowly unbuttoned my flannel and peeled it off my arms. My hard nipples poked through my bra and tank top, and the heat of his stare, the hunger in his dark eyes seeped wetness from between my thighs.

Tank top up and off.

Another groan.

I stood at the bed's edge, inches from his knees, and unclasped my bra behind my back, shucking it loose and shaking my breasts in the process.

"Fucking gorgeous." He trailed the back of his free hand over my breast while fucking his hand. "Gonna fuck those tits, vixen. Gotta have them."

"Later," I rasped, horny as hell and buzzing like mad. Forget letting him make me scream before filling me. My patience for him had run the fuck out. "I need your cock inside me. Now."

My damn boots… *Fuck stripping.*

I shoved against his chest, and he laid back, sweeping his thumb over the bead of pre-cum welling at the tip of his cock, a cocky, delicious smirk on his lips.

"Come and get it, hungry girl," he murmured, his dark eyes alight with life and lust enough to make my heart pound. "However you want it."

I wanted it alright—as deep as he could go.

"Gonna ride you in reverse," I told him while turning and grasping his thighs, "so I can feel you in the back of my throat." And because I couldn't afford to get caught up in emotions or have the patience to take off my boots and jeans wrapped right around my ankles.

"Fuck, yeah." He notched his thick head against my sopping pussy.

Lower lip between my teeth and eyes clenched shut, I sank down with a rush, impaling myself—filling myself to the womb with his thick length. We both cursed, and he grasped my hips with his huge hands to lift me up and slam me back down.

Yes… Holy fuck, yes.

I'd planned on doing all the work, giving my thighs a good workout, but he held me still and fucked in and out of me like we had two minutes to live.

"Christ, woman." He cursed again as though through clenched teeth. "Fucking tight and hot … so damn wet for my dick."

My boobs bounced, every thrust of his hips slamming him against my cervix and exploding stars behind my closed eyelids as whimpers leaked past my lips.

"Play with your clit," he said through clenched teeth. "I want to feel you cream all over me."

My hard nub throbbed, and at the first slide of my fingers against the aching flesh, I gasped and arched, seconds from coming.

He rose to meet me, his hot, hard chest against my back, arms wrapped around my body in a vise, holding me and bouncing me on his cock. "Can I fill you up, vixen? Fill you with my hot cum?"

"Fuck, yes."

"Then squeeze the life out of my dick with your sweet pussy. Give it to me," he whispered hotly against my ear and bit down on my lobe.

My core detonated, and I shrieked, every cell in my body pulsing with release. His hard thrusts, the lush drag of his thick length against my inner walls prolonged my climax. I whimpered, gasping for breath, while convulsing in his hold.

"Fuck, vixen." He clamped his mouth onto my neck and let out a deep groan, his cock pulsing and spurting cum deep inside me.

Holy fucking hell.

Sucking wind, I tipped my head back against his shoulder, but opened my eyes as the spins started up. I couldn't focus on the ceiling but couldn't bring myself to care. The rich boy's cock stayed hard inside me, his thumping heart against my back in perfect rhythm with mine as we came down.

He nibbled my neck where he'd probably left a hickey while unloading inside me, and a shudder rippled over my body.

Buzzing and sated for the moment, my heart began to thaw. Fucking emotions of feeling connected beyond the physical rose up because I had no control when under the influence.

Rich boy just passing through. No strings. No names, I reminded myself.

But hell, I liked him and could easily fall for his laid-back, confident personality. And his thick, fuckable cock? Oh, yeah.

"Who are you?" I murmured, blinking at the wavering ceiling.

"No one of importance."

"You fuck like a god."

He laughed and licked along my neck like he enjoyed the taste of my sweaty skin.

"Seriously, though. What are you doing in Alaska?" I pushed because buzzed Jessie liked to talk too damn much. "Where are you headed?"

"Thought we said no strings." A trace of annoyance laced his words, and I told myself to let it go. I'd agreed to one night only—couldn't let my hormones dictate the need for more. Shouldn't have had that damn third shot. Or was it forth?

Stupid.

"No strings," I forced out. I squeezed my inner walls around his semi, hoping to bring us both back to the fact the night wasn't yet over.

He released his tight hold on my torso to palm my breasts and lift them together. His dick jerked inside me as I squeezed him again, and he groaned while nuzzling beneath my ear. "Fuck, these tits."

I arched my back, smiling that he couldn't keep his hands off my best assets. "Not too big?"

He snorted. "Fuck, no."

His rolling of both my nipples at the same time pulsed my pussy around his length which lengthened deep inside me— just like I had wanted. My body revved for round two.

"Mmm." He gyrated his hips, letting me know he wasn't nearly done either even as our combined cum leaked from me. "Can I fuck these tits, vixen? Give me something to dream about and jerk off to tomorrow night?"

I'd met a few men who liked to talk dirty in bed, and I'd never been anything but embarrassed by their vocal inhibitions. But Mr. Rich Boy with the Boston accent? Hot. As. Hell.

I lifted off his cock, ignoring the rush of wetness running down my thighs.

He groaned and grabbed my hips before I could move. "Bend over and take off your boots."

Doing so would put my cum-covered pussy and thighs in his face—I guess that's what he wanted, because the second I bent to untie my hiking boots, he dove in like a starving man who'd been lost out in the bush. He held me steady, licking and sucking, drawing more arousal from me as I fought with my damn boot laces. Lapping up his own cum with mine—and groaning as though it was the best damn thing he'd ever tasted.

Dirty rich boy… I liked it. A lot.

He licked up my ass crack, tonguing my hole, his groans pulsing my pussy. "Fucking delicious."

I straightened as his hold loosened, kicked off my jeans, and crawled around him on the squeaky mattress to lean against the headboard, fighting to focus. "Come and get it," I repeated his words with a smirk, lifting my breasts and pushing them together even though I'd rather have his cock shoved deep inside me again.

"Damn." His dark eyes stayed glued to my breasts while he stood and rid himself of his boots and the rest of his clothes.

I hated that my damn eyesight hazed from my buzz, and I

blinked, trying to drink in my fill of tanned skin stretched tight over rippling muscles—wide shoulders, thick pecs, a for-real eight-pack of abs drawing in tight between a luscious V I wanted to suckle and bite.

He closed in, cutting off my view, but rose to his knees and grabbed the headboard. Our cum still glistened on his length, and he shoved up through the flesh valley I'd created with a groan. I lifted my breasts higher as he backed off, and his second glide through my flesh brought the tip of his cock within tongue reach. I flicked over the head, drawing another groan from his chest, and tightening his abs mere inches from my face.

"Fuck…" A few more thrusts, and I got a mouthful of cock, tasting the musk and saltiness of us both, my saliva giving him more lube to fuck between my breasts.

The headboard creaked beneath his grip, and he cursed again, his thrusts growing erratic. "Holy fuck, woman. I'm gonna come."

"Mmm," I said around a mouthful of his dick.

He pulled away from my lips, backed out of my breasts, and grasped his length, jerking. "Open your mouth, vixen. I want to shoot all over your gorgeous face."

I offered my breasts, but also leaned forward and opened my mouth like he'd told me to do.

Hot spunk exploded across my lips, and I closed my eyes, letting him shoot wherever the hell he wanted. My cheek. My neck. Between my breasts. Damn rope after rope of hot cum, like the man hadn't filled me minutes earlier.

"Goddamn."

I opened my eyes against the spins, struggling to focus on his face above me.

Dark eyes peered at me, sated of lust, but widened as

though full of wonder or some such shit. At least, that's what it looked like to my almost-drunk brain.

I giggled. "Jaws hanging open."

He snapped it shut.

"You going to clean this off me, too, or can we hop in the shower?"

A glint lit in his dark eyes. "Can I fuck you against the shower wall?"

"If you can get it up again."

His cocky grin did funny things to my insides, and I laughed, something I hadn't done freely in a long-ass time.

Turned out he could get it up again—and he fucked me against the shower wall, every grunt, every hard thrust of his hips plowing into me over and over until I came with a sob, thoroughly wrecked, thoroughly done.

I wanted more of my little rich boy. A hell of a lot more.

I passed the fuck out the second my head hit the pillow, only to wake in darkness with his face between my thighs, my head still pleasantly buzzed. The man was insatiable for all things Jessie, and when he flipped me onto my knees, stuffed me full with his cock and shoved his thumb in my ass, I groaned out curses rather than the name I wanted to know, tumbling headfirst into a gutter of lust and more.

Thankfully, I slept again before I thought too long on having to let him go come morning.

———

I woke like that Frozen princess, drool dangling from my lip, my eyes bleary as hell. Temples throbbing, I rolled with a groan, wiping my mouth, and blinking into focus the fact the bed beside me sat empty. The bathroom door hung open, the light off. An ache spread across my lower abdomen as I pushed up to sit, the sheet falling to my waist, and I grimaced in realization of the time of month.

Cramps—fucking lovely.

And my little rich boy had taken the fuck off. A quick glance around the room let me in on the fact he hadn't left a note, either.

"Fucking prick." Scowling, I tossed back the sheet and made my way to the bathroom. Sure enough, I'd gotten my damn period. Didn't have a pad or tampon with me, either. Letting out a long spew of curses, I stole one of the motel's towels, folded it into a makeshift pad, and shoved it against my leaking core while yanking up my panties.

My cell's alarm went off, and I grabbed it from my jeans back pocket, still not fully awake, still pissed he'd skipped, and I'd gotten my period. Shit day two, and it had only begun.

Forehead dented and lips pressed tight, I swiped my cell screen to life—and let out another string of *fucks* and *goddamnits*, grabbing my clothes and scurrying to dress.

An hour from home, from the airport, and I had fifteen minutes to get there for my morning appointment. "Fuck my life!" I grabbed my keys and hurried outside, stomping across the gravel lot, across the street toward the bar's parking area, flipping off an eighteen-wheeler who beat me there, making me five seconds later.

My piece of shit truck sat unmolested in Dale's lot, and I hopped in, praying the fucking thing didn't shit the bed.

At least one thing went right for me—it coughed to life and purred. Seconds later, I tore up the road, passing that damn eighteen-wheeler in a no-passing zone. The engine screamed under the hood, but I couldn't let up. I'd lost one customer the day before and couldn't afford to lose another.

I grabbed my cell to look up the guy's contact number to

let him know I'd be late—and found my cell dead as a drowned rat. A quick hunt around the console and glove compartment for the charger while flying up the road came up empty.

"Goddamnit!"

Cramps kept me curled around the steering wheel, and pissiness over being screwed because I'd had too much to drink, and ended up high and dry without a damn goodbye that morning kept my scowl firmly etched in place. I had fucked up but blamed the man who'd blown my mind the night before to make myself feel better.

Fucking rich boy. Prick. Got what he wanted and bailed.

The fact we had agreed to that very thing—that all I'd been in it for was a hard fuck to lessen the shit of the day— didn't lessen my annoyance. I hoped to come along that luscious prick on the highway just so I could run him off the road in my race to the airport.

5

BROCK

I gripped the steering wheel, lips in a tight line, brow furrowed. Fucking hated to leave Ms. Vixen like I had done, but I'd woke to find I had less than an hour to drive to the airport where my pilot waited to load up my shit and take me out to the bush. The first day in my new life, and I'd already fucked it up by oversleeping. The fact I'd slept for more than four hours straight didn't pass my notice, but I was too pissed off to care or focus on the fact it could have been having a soft, warm body beside mine that had helped.

My arm pits smelled like the deepest reaches of hell since I'd run out of that damn motel room like some psycho chased me with a fire poker, ready to brand my asshole. No time for a shower. No time for a shit and shave. No time for a quickie, one last taste—or even some fumbled words of goodbye or conversation over the fact I didn't want to say goodbye. I'd thrown on the clothes from the night before and grabbed my bag, but had paused in the doorway, needing one last glimpse to fuel my fantasies on the long, lonely nights ahead of me.

I'd never wanted a woman long term, but if I had, Ms. Vixen seemed the sort I would want. Funny. Driven. Vocal and sexually needy enough to sate my own needs that she'd woken from a two-year sleep. She'd been plaint in my arms, more giving rather than taking like I'd expected. Soft. Warm. Wet.

"Should have left a damn note," I growled at myself, glancing at my truck's clock for the tenth or so time. "Fuck." I hated being late. Hated feelings of regret almost as much.

I should have just finished my damn beer at The Watering Hole and called it a night rather than get mixed up with that little vixen. The scent of her clung to my nose—my fingertips, too, I noted while sniffing them. My dick hardened at the sweetness I thought I'd licked clean the night before. Shoving the three fingers I'd had deep in her pussy during the night into my mouth, I sought after a remnant of taste—and came away disappointed.

My scowl deepened.

New life. New beginning. That meant leaving her in the past and moving the fuck on. My chest ached, though. She'd been damn near perfect, and I wished we'd met under different circumstances.

"Fucking regret." My teeth clenched once more, and I drove the rest of the way in silence, stewing rather than riding the rushing wind of adrenaline I'd been looking forward to for months.

———

I pulled up to the airport's chain link fence twenty minutes late to find a padlock shut the place up tight as a virgin's asshole. Stomach twisting, I grabbed my sat phone, powered it up, and checked my email messages.

"Should have taken the time to email and let them know

you'd be late, asshole," I muttered to myself, scrolling through a dozen emails in my inbox.

Nothing from Midnight Sun.

I pulled up the phone number I'd never used but had in my contacts. Number went straight to a robotic voicemail recording, but I didn't bother leaving one.

"Fuck." I tossed my cell aside and clenched the steering wheel again, staring out over the air strip and the two small hangars. A couple of planes sat around the property, two on floats rather than wheels docked in the river beyond. One of those had to belong to Midnight Sun since I'd been informed from the guy I'd bought the cabin off of that the river a hundred yards or so from the homestead acted as the landing strip.

I tried the phone number again, left a message that time, and ended up writing up an email in the hopes the owner of the small one-man-show checked his email before long if he couldn't get his cell powered up.

Unsure what the fuck to do, I settled in for a wait, and rather than let my thoughts linger on the woman I'd left behind, I checked my other messages. One from mom with a sob emoji begging me to be careful and to come home soon.

Adam, Garret, Rian, and Jordan had all also texted me after I'd said my goodbyes the night before, best wishes, take cares, and all that usual bullshit people spouted when one set off on a new adventure. Thank fuck none of them or their wives had been with me on that fateful trip up to Nova Scotia. Bad enough I'd killed my prick of a brother's fiancé, but if I'd been the one responsible for my non-blood brothers' wives' demise… No amount of therapy would have helped me move on. Not that I'd made great steps toward doing so anyway.

The deepest parts of me didn't feel worthy of forgiveness,

love, or even companionship, and I'd slowly been pushing my best friends away. I hadn't opened up about the shit in my head since Old Betsy had gone down, and knowing me and my despise of nosiness, they hadn't pushed. But, living their own happily-ever-afters, they had other things to focus on rather than a friend struggling to find meaning with his life two years after tragedy.

Rian, an FBI agent, had helped with the investigation over the affair. I'd been sued, and if not for his involvement in bringing Old Betsy's malfunction to light, I'd have gone down in a whole other way.

He'd offered proof the accident wasn't actually my fault —but my conscious didn't see it that way.

I didn't text back to my friends, turning my focus on the supply checklist I'd memorized in my head to get *out* of my damn head. Every five minutes, I checked my phone hoping for an email. It didn't come, and I began the process of turning my mind on other ways to get to my homestead. I'd paid top dollar for the smaller fish in the sea because the big time charter service out of Fairbanks I'd spoken to first was owned by a cocky prick, but I pulled up his website and considered putting the call through to see if he could get me out there in the next day or two.

"Don't have time for this shit," I grumbled and decided to call Midnight Sun again. No fucking answer. I tossed my cell onto the passenger seat.

I'd already set up the storage of my truck at the locked-up airport—paid for six months in advance, non-refundable, too since they usually didn't do that shit. Heading back to Fairbanks meant needing to make other arrangements, getting a hotel, and waiting out the time until I could get to my homestead.

"Or the fucking owner could just show up—"

A truck roared into the drive behind me, and grumbling a "Thank fuck," I hopped out, grimacing at my aching knee from being shut up and still for over an hour.

The beat-up Ford spit up dust, and I brushed the haze from my face, peering at the cab—my hand paused, dropping to my side as the driver came into view.

Ms. Vixen stared at me through the windshield, her small hands gripping her steering wheel, her eyes glacial. That instant connection I'd felt kicked me in the groin, but my forehead dented in a frown as thoughts flitted through my head. *Stalker? Wanting to kill me for leaving without a word? How the hell did she find me?*

Thought she'd only wanted the one night, too. What the fuck had I gotten myself into?

She squeaked open her door and stepped out, blonde hair a riotous mess, tousled like she'd been fucked three ways from Sunday—which she had.

My dick woke the hell up, and even though I wondered what the fuck was up, I couldn't help the smirk tugging on my lips at the fire in her eyes or the way her chest heaved as she stalked toward me. "Are you fucking kidding me?" she spit out, hands on her hips as she stopped in front of me, those cold, blue eyes knifing over my face. "Brock Charran?"

I opened my mouth to ask how she got my name, but the truth of the matter smacked me in the face even though her hands stayed put. My smile faded. "Jessie Blacke," I muttered. My conquest of the night was the bush pilot I'd been emailing on and off for months. I'd assumed Jessie was a man—my fucking bad.

"Fuck. My. Life." She stalked back to her truck, yanked out the keys, and strode past me—avoiding me by a good three feet—and unlocked the padlock while I stared.

"Fucking rich prick. Unfit for my wilderness," she muttered, yanking the chain free.

I shouldn't have cared she lumped me into the same category of that asshole who'd shit on her the day before, but I did—and her judgment pissed me the hell off. "Just because I fed you my dick last night, you think you know me? You don't know jack shit about me."

"I know too much," she shot back, turning to stare me down. "Including the size of that dick you're packing."

"Seemed to like it last night," I said, still scowling but grabbing myself through my pants and thrusting—hoping to piss her off.

The action did. Cold fire shot from her eyes as her forehead dented into a deeper frown. "Did you get what you wanted, Mr. Rich Man?"

Not nearly enough. My insides twisted up in some sort of fucked up lust/anger war, and I didn't know what the fuck to feel. "I got my one night, no strings attached before heading off into the wilderness, so yeah."

I also got a taste of the pussy that would haunt me for fucking life, too.

"Typical rich asshole." She brushed passed me again muttering something under her breath about taking off without a goddamn goodbye.

"What's that?" I called after her, every cell in my body like a live wire, ready to throw down—or go down. Fucking sexy as hell woman, bristling with indignation, pissy and flush-faced did a number on my balls, and my dick wept for another taste.

"I said I should have known better!" she spat the words over her shoulder. "Blue plane down by the dock—if you're still in need of a pilot!"

She hopped in her truck and tore around mine through the gate, kicking up more dust with her old Ford's tires.

Fuck. Me.

I scrubbed a hand down over my face, a shadow of whiskers the beginnings of a beard I planned on growing out in the coming months. My balls ached, dick fully erect and straining, wanting to bury between her thighs again. Hell, I even wanted her spitting and clawing, full of piss and vinegar. Would be one hell of a fuck.

"Damn her."

I followed after Jessie like she had me on a goddamn leash, thoughts of heading back to Fairbanks long gone.

6

JESSIE

S hit day number two couldn't get worse. Waking to cramps and finding out the best lay of my life hadn't felt the connection I did the night before, then finding out I had to spend a few hours in his company—close proximity in my old Beaver—to take him out into the bush pissed me off.

Well, I hoped said bush kicked his ass within twenty-four hours. I hoped his soft, rich ass used to being catered to pussied out at the first howl of a wolf or growl of a bear. I hoped the lack of people, the lack of noise, and anything else to distract one's mind drove him insane.

Literally.

My ragging ass wanted to tell him to fuck off. Wanted to tell him to go find some other pilot to cart his royal hind-ass around, but I needed his business. Telling him to take a hike would send him back to Fairbanks and Cort, I didn't doubt since he was the closest one around. Couldn't have that shit.

I counted myself lucky Brock followed me into the airport rather than turn around from the shit I'd spewed at him. It was a tiny place, owned by old man Foster who allowed only a handful of people access to keys. He entrusted the keep of the place to me which meant I got to dock my plane rent free.

I'd already emailed Brock the maximum weight my old plane could carry, and he'd emailed me back that weight wouldn't be an issue. The land and cabin he'd bought from Raymond after his father had died came fully furnished, most of the tools a homesteader would need included in the sale. Raymond had only taken a few trinkets as memories from the cabin when I'd flown him out there the fall before to shut the place down for the winter.

Brock Charran had paid top dollar for the homestead, but from his attire and the shiny, new truck he drove, I expected the cost hadn't put a dent in his bank account. Asshole probably had more than one, probably all overseas, too. Investments out the ass. He might live out in the bush but had the funds to blow on whatever he felt he needed to survive out there.

Scowl fixed firmly in place, I ignored him while readying my plane. Other than a few words about packing his shit behind our seats, I kept my lips sealed. The lack of conversation, however, didn't keep my lower lips sealed. Even on the rag, my body wanted him. Nipples strained and ached anytime he got within two feet of me. Damn breath even caught.

Pissed me off all the more.

Luckily, I kept a stash of woman shit in the bathroom off the tiny office old man Foster rarely visited anymore. If I'd had cash to spare, I'd have bought him out. But, unlike Brock Charran, I *didn't* have funds to spare. Not even for a coffee I desperately needed or the stack of bills back home on my kitchen table.

Stuffed full of cotton to keep me in the clear for the next couple of hours, a few ibuprofen from the medicine cabin swallowed down, a couple of Foster's granola bars in hand, and old muck boots to keep my feet dry, I headed back outside, steeling myself.

Focus on the money. The business. You need him, so play nice.

He'd parked his truck in the back of the hangar where Foster had agreed to, and I locked that up tight before ambling over to Brock waiting by my Beaver, his gaze on the mountains. Wide shoulders gave way to a trim waist, and an ass I'd wrapped my heels around during the night.

Memories of his mouth, the taste of his sweet breath, the slide of his tongue along mine sent an ache through my core —and clenched my teeth.

Damn traitorous body.

He turned as I neared, his dark eyes flitting down over me. While his frown had long since disappeared, I refused to budge in being cordial, leaving him to his self while I did my pre-flight check.

The second he settled into the cockpit beside me, the scent of male who'd fucked all night long and didn't shower slid over me. I should have been turned off, but the opposite effect tingled through me. Energy crackled in the small space between us, causing my hands to shake as I put on my headset and readied to take off.

Brock sat silent, hands on his thighs as though unaffected by being shut up in tight quarters with a woman he'd fucked all night long.

Bastard.

Those hands tightened as I took to the sky, knuckles turning white.

Afraid of flying? I glanced over to find his face a sickly pallor.

"You okay?" I asked, for a split second forgetting I hated

him, real concern in my mind. I told myself it was because I didn't want his puke all over my baby Beaver.

"Fine," he bit out through clenched teeth. "How long?"

"Little less than a half-hour." I banked northward, trying to push away my concern. I didn't want to know why he hated flying. Didn't care. At least, I told myself that, anyway. A part of me longed to know him inside and out—what made him tick, why he headed into the wilderness away from people, why his hands remained clenched on his thighs throughout our silent flight.

I also told myself it was my usual nosiness, not true interest in the man himself.

He obviously faced a fear being in the air in a small float plane, a fear I'd never had and couldn't understand. Freedom stretched as far as the eye could see, memories of Dad sitting alongside me, his gentle encouragement and chides over how I flew ringing in my ears.

An ache spread through my chest as it often did when in the air, but I refused to get all emotional with the rich prick beside me. Fuck, I hated that concern once more slammed into me.

"Scared of flying?" I heard myself ask, lacking the contempt tone I'd given all morning.

"No." Snipped answer.

Prick got what he wanted and had no use for me beyond being his damn air chauffeur. Fine.

Temptation to take him for a thrill ride rose, but I squashed it down. We had turbulence enough, every jolt of the beast we sat inside tightening his hold on his thighs. I wasn't that much of a bitch.

"Knuckles are white," I muttered, not really wanting to know why. Who the fuck was I kidding? Pissiness at myself overrode what I felt toward him.

He didn't respond.

"Better get that fear in check, rich boy," I said, refusing to look at him. "This is nothing compared to what you'll face out there."

"I'm not afraid."

I snorted. He had no fucking clue what he could encounter out in my world. Spoiled and pampered, I expected he'd be radioing me to haul his ass out of there before winter settled in. If he didn't haul ass out of there with me when I flew in to deliver the supplies we'd already scheduled for October.

Five months. I would drop Brock off at his cabin beside the river and fly off, not to see him again for that length of time. Another ache pinged in my chest, but different than the grief I still felt over losing my parents. I wasn't sure what the feeling was and why it brought up emotion to clog my throat.

Did I really like a man I'd only just met?

I glanced over to find him peering out the window beside him, not offering me much of a view of his face beyond his scruffy jaw which appeared clenched and the short hair buzzed around the back of his ear. In five months, he'd be fully bearded, his hair curling around that ear.

Warmth returned between my thighs, full force. Bearded, burly bush man? Especially one with eyes as dark as Brock's and a dick that would without a doubt be aching for a woman after months away from humanity? A dick, hands, and tongue that would be fueling my fantasies and dreams?

Yes, please.

I cleared my throat rather than curse into the headset where he would hear—and perhaps question why I swore out of the clear blue.

Damn him.

7

BROCK

My first time in flight in two years—and I felt bile rising along with the muffin I'd had left over from the baker in Fairbanks from the morning before that I'd kept overnight in my truck. I held onto my thighs to keep from shaking as my heart raced and dizziness plagued my damn head.

I'd never passed out in my life and wouldn't allow my conscious the rest, especially sitting beside a woman who would get a kick out of my showing weakness. Keeping my jaw clenched and running through my to-do list for the first couple days at my escape helped to keep nightmarish memories away.

Water collection.

Solidify shelter.

Firewood.

Food wouldn't be an issue for the first few weeks, but until the seeds I'd brought along for a garden sprouted, and I managed to get some wild game to roast over a fire, canned goods and the sourdoughs starter I'd brought for biscuits would have to do.

Every move Jessie made sent a whiff of vanilla and woman past my nose, offering distraction from the chores ahead of me. Focusing on her, on the live-wire energy between us, put my already on edge nerves on high alert.

The old "fight or flight" adage rose to mind as my body warred with wanting to do both with the little vixen. But a plane's cockpit locked me in, and I couldn't control my body's desire for the woman beside me.

I should have been soaking in the sights—the rising mountains still showcasing snow on their sides and peaks, the sprawling pines below, the winding river in the distance—but all I could think about when not breathing Jessie into my lungs was the tailspin and the high speed landing I'd had no choice but to attempt.

And failed.

Jessie banked toward our left, dipping my stomach clear down to my fucking toes, and leveled back out, slowly descending while I fought PTSD, sweat beading on my upper lip and forehead.

"Two-o'clock." She spoke without a bite in her tone, her husky voice bringing me thoroughly to the present.

I focused on the river below, my gaze flitting up the bank toward where she'd said.

My cabin. My escape, and hopefully, the place of finding myself and true peace once more.

A grin broke out over my face, and I leaned forward, adrenaline replacing the souring bile in the blink of an eye.

I expected Jessie to land without preamble, but she buzzed the clearing, giving me a spectacular bird's eye view of my new home. On a whole, forty acres, but only two sat fully cleared along the river, towering pines behind.

"There's no dock," I noted, checking along shore.

"Log ramp."

Not exactly an explanation, but I didn't concern myself. Midnight Sun had been the old man's supplier before I'd bought the place. I expected Jessie knew what she was doing. She banked again, and I kept my focus on the cabin while she prepared to land on the river. The second the floats dragged in the water, the plane jolted, and I grabbed hold on the top of the dashboard with both hands, images of the ground rushing up to meet me and Old Betsy flashing in jagged memories.

Jessie didn't laugh, didn't spare me a glance, as I swallowed against the damn muffin wanting to spew past my lips.

If nothing else, the fear of flying back to civilization would keep me in the bush. One therapist had suggested flying to help face my fear, but all it had done was take me to the verge of puking and soaking my shirt with sweat.

An old log ramp secured to shore and disappeared into the water directly in front of the cabin, just like Jessie had said, and she pulled right up like an old pro. We'd had a quiet flight in both noise and trouble. The woman knew what she was doing, without doubt. Bush pilots were noted to be the best there were, and even though I doubted she'd hit thirty years of age, she'd flown like she'd been born to it.

I waited for her to shut down and hop out before following. In continued silence, we tied up both floats to the ramp's top, and I turned to take in my new beginning. A few dozen yards up a rocky path lay the cabin, spring's new leafage and growth creating a sea of green and early, tiny flowers in a picturesque setting. Woods expanded from the back, leading to the hills and mountain pass beyond, and fluffy white clouds lazed overhead.

The scent of pine, earth, and the river filled my lungs as I dragged oxygen in deep until I felt close to bursting. Lapping water. Chirping birds. A chattering squirrel or similar creature. The shriek of a bird of prey who soared overhead. And utter man-made silence.

No buzz of distant traffic. No hum of aircraft far overhead.

Pure nature lay like a soothing blanket over my surroundings.

I'll find peace here. I will.

My feet itched to check out the cabin, but the sound of the plane's door opening pulled me away from my heaven on earth. Jessie went right to work, pulling some of my shit out of the back of the plane and bringing it to shore to drop a few feet from where I stood.

I followed her to the plane rather than take off exploring, my knee loosening with every step. She wasn't there to spend the day with me while I acquainted myself with my new home. She'd been paid to fly me out and drop me off. Period. And the way she hurried, you'd think she hated my guts and wanted to escape my presence as quick as possible—which her coldness seemed to indicate, too.

At least she helped me unload. Probably so she could take off and leave me behind faster.

"Closest people are just shy of ten miles over that ridge and through the pass," Jessie surprised me by saying as we carried our second arm load ashore.

I glanced toward the mountain beyond my cabin where she'd indicated with her chin.

"Backwoods type," she continued. "The man's woman passed, or so I heard, and he's taken up with his daughter."

"Taken up, taken up?" I asked, my eyebrow shooting upward while I swiped my forearm across my sweaty brow.

Jessie set the box down on the rocky shore and shrugged before heading back to the plane. "Don't know, don't care. He's no longer my problem."

Her tone indicated she hated the prick as much as she hated me.

I didn't ask.

While the temperature couldn't be more than sixty or so, I always ran hot, and stripped off my sweat-stained shirt before heading back to the plane.

Awareness of Jessie's nearness heated me almost as much as the excursion of unloading boxes and supplies. I didn't catch her checking me out, but I felt her gaze as clearly as if she caressed me with her fingers—but I was guilty of the same, snagging an eyeful of her curvy body whenever I could, memorizing every dip and swell beneath the clothing she'd stripped off for me the day before, the way her hair fluttered in the breeze, and how she constantly tucked the white-blonde strands behind her ears.

Missing having a female beneath me hadn't been high on my mind's thought priority—until Jessie. I considered attempting to bridge whatever shit wall she held to keep me at a distance, but I also didn't want her knowing my past and judging me. I would be less than bird shit in her pilot's eyes if she knew why I'd decided to hide away.

We finished unloading in silence, and she shut the plane up, readying for takeoff.

I expected her to hop into the cockpit without uttering another peep, but she climbed back up the ramp and stuck out her hand, her eyes glacial and shut off.

"Good luck, Brock."

Wrapping my hand around hers sent a shot of pure lust to my dick and had me wanting to drag her against my bare chest and devour her pouty lips even though I stank like rotten onions. I expected a good right hook to land on my nose if I attempted any such action. Keeping things professional like her offering her hand, I nodded and released my hold.

"Safe trip back," I said. "I'll call you in September to update my supply list—if you still plan on making the trip out here this fall."

She hesitated long enough I wondered what the fuck went through her head and if I'd fucked myself by fucking her. "Just let me know what you need."

Another night—two nights—with you beneath me. Your scent surrounding me, your body a welcome, wet glove sucking me deep, giving me something to bury my soul inside.

I clenched my jaw against telling her the truth of what I wanted, and she turned away, the sway of her hips and thick thighs my focal point. All woman. Lush and delicious. Sassy, confident, and hot as hell. An adjustment to my dick became necessary, and I took care of business before she finished untying her plane from the ramp. She didn't turn or call a goodbye but climbed into the cockpit as though I didn't exist.

The engine roared to life, and she backed off the ramp, her gaze finally flitting toward me through the open side window. From the distance between us, I couldn't make out her eyes—what she might be feeling or thinking.

I lifted a hand in farewell, my excitement waning as she took to the air without returning the gesture, leaving me alone on land.

Jessie didn't buzz the clearing again but headed back the way we'd come—away from me, as though she couldn't create distance between us fast enough.

8

───────

JESSIE

The scent of Brock lingered in my nose long after I left him behind, and I cursed myself for being such a bitch. I was the last soul he would see until summer's end. I'd half expected him to ask me to stay for a while—fuck one last time which I probably could have been talked into regardless of his needing a shower and the fact I was on the rag—but that cabin on the hill held his attention even as we'd unpacked.

I knew he wanted to get up there and make his home. He hadn't spared me a glance, making me feel as though I didn't exist. He'd gotten what he wanted.

So did I, I told myself. *A night I'll never forget.*

That strange ache settled into my chest again as I flew out of his cabin's sight. Had he watched me leave, or had he immediately strode up the path the second I took off, all thoughts of me and our night together lost in the adventure ahead of him? I'd wanted to buzz over, wave with a dip of my wings, but he didn't deserve more than he'd paid for.

We'd fucked, but that didn't make him my friend. I'd been a means to an end for him, one last hurrah before solitude in the wilderness, and I'd do best to remember that fact. I tended to always use my head rather than my heart but spending the night with Brock had shifted something deep inside me. I hated the feeling of not being the one in control of my thoughts and emotions. I hated that he held sway over my libido.

The only way to keep my future safe was if I stayed in control and having Brock Charran a flight away from my daily life would make it easier.

I hoped.

I definitely couldn't take any risks, and wanting more with a man like him would only invite danger.

My cramps returned full force, deepening my frown. A shitty day all around. At least I was free of Brock Charran until October. I could stand on my own two feet rather than cave to the need to sprawl on my back or drop to my knees if he breathed my way.

Leaving that little rich boy out in the wilderness without a backwards glance was the best thing you could have done.

My throat tightened and eyes hazed over, making me question what I told myself.

"Damn period," I grumbled to myself. That fucking thing needed to end just as much as Cort's pursuit of me.

Maybe I'd look into that shot that rid a woman of dripping for a few months.

Maybe I'd invite Cort over for dinner and put a bullet through his brain the second he walked into my small home, too.

The first could be easily done, but I snorted at the second thought. Putting Cort down would land me in a heap load of shit considering who his cousin was and the police department at his back.

I needed to stay away from Fairbanks. I also needed to set

aside thoughts of Brock. Enough stress waited for me at home, namely the bills I had no money to pay. Thinking about one man, let alone two, needed to stop.

"I'll keep my own two feet beneath me and build our family name back up, Dad. One way or another."

Tears didn't prick my eyes for the first time while speaking to him in flight, and I tipped my chin upward, readying to land back at old man Foster's dock.

I would make it on my own and reap the pride in accomplishing my task without the help of a man. Thoughts of Brock trickled back in, but I pushed those aside as well. I didn't need him, either.

Just sure as hell wanted him.

It was going to be a long summer.

9

BROCK

The single-story log cabin looked sturdy enough with logs peeled to ward off rot, its sod roof atop rubber matting that had been replaced two years earlier sprouted grass and weeds, attempting to blend man's shelter into nature. A washboard and a few other ancient tools that looked to still be in working order hung on the side wall, the roof's two-foot overhang protecting them from the elements. Maybe a half-cord of firewood stacked against the other wall, unsplint logs scattered in a pile a little ways away beside a three-sided shelter where the old man must have stacked firewood to keep it out of the rain and snow. An outhouse sat on its other side.

South-facing windows flanked the cabin's door, and I stuck my half-eaten protein bar between my teeth I'd chewed on while walking up the trail to dig the padlock's key I'd picked up from the old man's son in Fairbanks from my back pocket. A bird chirped from the roof, and I tilted my head back to find a chickadee watching me with its beady little eyes.

I snagged the protein bar from my mouth. "Hey, there," I said, my voice loud in the stillness.

He chirped again, unmoved by my nearness, shifting and tilting his head like he sized me up.

"You can have the insects around here," I told him, "but the berries are mine."

Unfazed, he peered at me while I bit off a bite of my bar.

"Want some?" I crumbled a piece off the uneaten corner and held it out on my palm.

He hopped a foot to the side, head swiveling, while I held still.

Another chirp, and he launched down, snatched the offering, and took off in a flutter of wings.

Must have been the old man's buddy to be that ballsy.

Grinning, I unlocked the padlock and pushed in the cabin's door. No scent of mold or mildew met my nose, but staleness from disuse lay beyond. Two windows on the eastern wall helped those on the front to allow me to see once my eyes adjusted to the dim interior.

I stepped over the threshold and took the place in, my stupid grin fixed in place while I chewed the last of my so-called lunch.

A bed box in the far left corner looked sturdy enough—and fucking hard as hell with planks for its platform rather than weaved ropes. Until I stuffed the tick I'd brought along with dried grasses, a hard bed it would be.

A work bench roughly two feet deep spanned the entire wall on my right with shelving above. The rock fireplace against the far wall appeared blackened with use, a rough-hewn log mantle embedded above showcased old snowshoes. A small wood stove on the left had a flat top for cooking. Thank fuck for the various pieces of cast iron hung on nails behind the stove—bringing those supplies would have maxed out the weight limit for Jessie's plane.

The square table tucked against the wall between the stove and bed box had a single chair beneath it, both obviously handmade, an old oil lamp sitting in the middle. Another sat on a small stand beside the bed. I'd brought a bit of oil since the lamps had been on the list of supplies included in my purchase.

Simplistic and yet all a man needed to survive. The portable solar panel charger I'd brought would be more than enough to keep my sat phone up and running for emergencies, but other than that one tie to humanity, solitude settled over me.

A deep sense of contentment, *almost* peace, sat on my shoulders as I labored to get all of my shit up to the cabin, the chance to move rather than stay shut up in my truck allowing my old injury from the crash to mellow the fuck out. Therapy had done all it could, but when cramped up for long periods, or in intense cold, the fucking thing flared, causing me to limp.

I refused my one physical weakness to dictate my survival in the wilderness. I refused my mental weakness the same, thankful the lack of people where I'd chosen to live out my life would make that aspect easier.

Twice, the chickadee hopped on the front door's overhanging roof, chirping. Both times, I offered another nibble of my second protein bar, deciding I liked his company—could definitely live with it.

"Don't get used to it, kid," I told him about the snacks as he fluttered off to nearby brush. "I'm done being responsible for anyone but myself."

Sweat dripped off me, and I chugged the bitter cold river water down, dunking my head beneath the surface twice and getting brain freeze. Without plumbing, it would be a cold river bath until the winter months when I would be forced to heat water for sponge baths. Body odor would be my new best friend, but that didn't mean I had to live like a pig.

I'd brought enough eco-friendly soap bars to keep me clean for the next six months and dilutable laundry bars. While I planned on becoming a mountain man in every sense of the word, I had no wish to revert to my instinctual animal ways living in grime and filth.

Four hours later, a can of cold stew in my stomach and all my supplies unpacked, I headed out to the three-sided shop of sorts the old man had set up beside the outhouse. He'd left behind an axe, but unsure of its state, I'd brought a new one along.

Shelter all set, water brought up from the river in collapsible water containers, and it was time to focus on the firewood, the chore that topped my daily to-do list. Enough split wood sat against the house for immediate use to heat the cabin at night, but building up my supply for the long winter ahead would be the main focus of my summer as well as the garden I would set to work on the following day. A man could never have too much firewood—better to be safe than sorry. I figured I'd split over the coming months until I felt I had enough, then split another two cords to play it safe.

I'd been an avid gym member for years, trying to regain my leg's full strength and strain the guilt and anger out of my insides by punishing my outside, so I didn't fear hard work. I attacked the cut logs with vigor, eating up the burn, the ache that eventually settled into my muscles from every swing of the axe. With my downward strokes, I imagined splitting my survivor's guilt in two, leaving the emotion cleaved, broken down to better deal with.

If only ridding my head of it came as easy as my axe blade ate away at the wood.

A fire crackled in the fireplace that night, fighting off the cooler temperatures settling in even though darkness didn't truly cover the land. All shut up, snug as a bug in a damn rug after a cold as fuck bath in the river, I laid on top of the blankets in my bed box, not caring of its hardness. Exhaustion pulled on my eyelids along with a slight ache in my knee, and I settled my eyes closed, loving the feeling of accomplishment in my head.

Only day one, and I already felt as though I'd come miles from where my head had been back home. I doubted I would ever find true peace, but perhaps I'd find a bit. Contentment and pride of accomplishment came easy, but self-esteem and worth beyond survival abilities lagged.

Forgiveness of self, my last therapist had claimed, was pertinent to psychological well-being, but all the meditation, focusing, admitting mistakes out loud, imagining myself as someone I could love she had encouraged… None of it came easy. None of it had seemed to help, either.

The tears of people whose loved ones I'd killed, the blame spewed from my brother's lips, had lodged in the deepest parts of me. I wasn't worthy of his forgiveness, wasn't worthy of his friendship. Even though we shared blood, I was no longer his brother. Cut off, a vast valley between us that our parents hadn't been able to bridge.

"Fuck." I pinched the bridge of my nose.

Recognizing I needed to get back into the present, I focused on the fact I'd bathed in frigid waters, smelled better, and had a roof over my head. If only I had a warm body atop mine. Memories of Jessie's soft tits flooded my mind and my mouth with drool. Within seconds, my dick swelled, ready and leaking.

Who needed lotion when pre-cum oozed to slicken my hand's strokes? I lost my thoughts to Jessie, to her flashing eyes, and smirk. I remembered her whimpers, her husky moans—and groaned her name as spunk shot up over my chest.

So much for being clean.

At least pure exhaustion pulled me under, releasing my conscious mind.

10

JESSIE

Two weeks of non-shitty days passed. Two weeks of silence at the hangar and home except when taking a couple tourists out for a joy ride and dropping spring supplies at Callan Kelly's place, another client north of Brock's place.

He visited me nightly in my mind, either giving me something to masturbate to, or waking me up horny, aching, and pissed off. My emotion's focus stayed honed in on the negative, his lack of attention the morning after, rather than the words and touches my body remembered all-too well. The pissiness at him remained, and I clung to it like a stubborn bitch, so I wouldn't miss him. I kidded myself, though, thoroughly caught up in thoughts about a man I hardly knew.

I blew a steady breath out through my nose and returned to the books old man Foster kept on his desk. Not only had I taken over the upkeep and care of his lot, I'd also taken over keeping his finances straight. I feared dementia set in, and with his only blood having taken off to California a dozen years earlier, never mind his good treatment of me, I felt responsible for him.

His finances were a hell of a lot better off than mine, but

payment had come in for one of my clients I'd taken a second trip to supply, covering those damn bills I'd been worried over.

In the clear—for the time being.

Double checking my math for his monthly expense report, I experienced jealousy over the fact Foster's kids would inherit his business fully. Foster didn't gamble. Didn't get drunk like my dad had done on occasion and make stupid mistakes.

An engine rumbled, pulling my focus off the spreadsheet in front of me, and I glanced out the window.

A black Escalade pulled alongside my truck.

Fucking Cort Endsley.

"What the hell is he doing here?" I grumbled, hopping up from behind the desk.

A mechanic worked in the hangar across from me, the door wide open, his back in plain sight. I wasn't about to get shut up in a room with Cort, so I hurried out into the bright sunlight to confront him in a semi-public place.

"What are you doing here?" I called out, getting the mechanic's attention, too, as I'd intended.

Cort didn't sport his usual twinkling eyes and lazy grin when meeting my glare while approaching, and a tingle of unease slid down my spine as he drew closer.

"Jessie."

I fought the need to tuck my arms around myself and lifted my chin as he stopped a few feet away from me. "What are you doing here?" I repeated, thankful my voice remained steady.

"Have something here for you." He held out an envelope.

I snatched it from him, frowning like mad at my shaking hands as I ripped it open.

Notification of a lawsuit…

Trademark infringement…

"What the fuck?"

"Midnight Sun Charter is mine." Satisfaction laced his voice, along with the contempt that had him threatening me before.

"The fuck it is," I shot back, glaring up at him and crumpling the legal papers in my hand.

"Not your little DBA," Cort amended, glancing at my Beaver docked in the river, "but the name itself."

"You don't own the fucking name, you asshole," I snipped.

His smirk as he returned his focus on my face twisted my insides. "I trademarked the LLC after gaining control from your father."

I stared, processing what he claimed. "Why the fuck would you do that? You already own a charter service of your own."

Cort's eyes hardened, glinting an icy blue, as his lips flatlined. "Once upon a time, he wouldn't give me what I wanted. Well, I took what was most precious to him and made it my own."

I won't give him what he wants—and now he wants to take what is most precious to me.

"You fucking bastard," I spit the words, wishing the daggers in my eyes could slice through his fancy button-down shirt, through the flesh and bone beneath.

His sudden flash of teeth and grin didn't meet his eyes. "It doesn't have to be this way, Jessie. Give me what I want, and I'll drop the lawsuit." He moved closer in a cloud of expensive cologne, vibrating my entire body with need to punch his nose clear into his brain. "Learn from your father's mistake—agree to be mine, and I'll cancel the trademark. You can legally own Midnight Sun Charter without my interference."

One fuck, one spread of the legs, and I could be rid of the fucker.

Too bad the thought of his dick within two feet of me heaved my stomach.

Needing those two feet, I stepped back, but didn't show an ounce of fear on my face or in my stance. "Not happening, Cort. I'll find a lawyer and fight you on this until the day I die."

His entire face darkened, and I took another step back, my muscles tight with need to preserve myself from the monster lurking in his eyes.

"You look like your father, but you're a dumb cunt, just like your mother."

My head jerked back as though he'd slapped me, and I stared, gaping as he spun and stomped back to his Escalade.

My mother. How the fuck had he even known my mother? Why the hell would he even say such a thing? She'd been a saint, admired by everyone in our small town. Helped those with newborns, those sick, and whoever ended up stuck in bed.

Tears stung my eyes as Cort whipped out of the lot, kicking up dust and pebbles. The cloud of his exit drifted over me as I stared after him.

"Jessie?"

I turned to find the mechanic approaching, his gaze flitting toward Cort's vehicle and back to me again, concern in his eyes.

"You okay?"

"Y-yeah." I forced a wobbling smile even as tears slid down my cheeks. "Yeah." A clearing of my throat didn't help to cease my tears or my churning stomach. "I'm fine."

My legs wooden, I turned around before he could question further, and somehow managed to make it back to Foster's desk without collapsing.

Lawsuit.

Cunt.

A sob ripped loose, and I clasped a hand over my mouth, smoothing out the legal papers with my other hand so I could give them a thorough read. It didn't take me long to realize one thing quite clearly.

Unless I willingly spread my legs for Cort Endsley, I would lose my business name. Fail my father and our family name.

I'm fucked. Royally.

BROCK

I watched the hairy fucking beast on the ridge above my cabin through my binoculars for a few days, his slow descent looking for shit to eat after waking from hibernation bringing him too damn close to my home for comfort. While out hunting small game, my nerves sat raw, my senses alert. Every snap of a twig not caused by my own feet sent a shot of adrenaline through my blood.

But not the type I usually enjoyed.

I'd hoped being forced to live in somewhat close proximity to grizzly bears would help me conquer my discomfort of being around the only animal to stand my neck hairs on end.

No such fucking luck.

I kept my pistol and knife on my hips and a rifle slung over my shoulder whenever I explored beyond my clearing. For six weeks, I hadn't run across more than a handful of moose—too big to take down for food since I didn't have a freezer.

Fishing salmon proved good, though, and I smoked and packed away countless pounds for the winter ahead. Radishes and early beets had sprouted, and I devoured the greens whenever harvesting their leaves wouldn't hinder root growth.

The damn grizzly fished down river one morning, too damn close to where I always took my morning dip of a bath, and I forced myself to sit a hundred yards or so away from him in attempts to get over myself. He eyed me with contempt, but made no move to charge me, merely went about his gathering of food.

"You just keep to yourself," I called to him, "and we won't have an issue."

He tossed his head as though I disturbed his peace.

Bastard sure as hell did the same to me, putting me on a knife-like edge I didn't know how to deal with.

That afternoon, once he disappeared, I kept vigilant while chopping and stacking wood, my gaze flitting away from my work more than was safe. Fucking heart in my throat, my nape tingled… I was a fucking mess.

I swung the axe, a shifting in the brush beside me jerking my focus off the log. The axe glanced off the wood and embedded in my boot, sinking into flesh and bone, and ripping a roar from my chest.

"Goddamnit! Fucking hell!" My holler echoed through the valley, and I clenched my jaw against the pain, all thoughts of Griz long fucking gone.

Curses ran through my head as I hobbled to the cabin, blood squishing in my boot.

"Oh, fuck. Fuck." I sat in my lone chair, heaving for breath, sweaty as hell, and tore my boot off. Blood dripped onto the floor from my sock.

I dreaded what I would find.

A slow peeling away of my soaked sock made a mess on the floor and revealed I'd been luckier than I thought. No bones protruded, and I could wiggle my toes, but the fucking thing bled like a gutted pig, the bit of flesh on my foot's outside dangling by a hair.

Sharp axes were all good and well in the bush, but my fear had caused a serious mishap, one that could very well end my stint in the wilderness.

Teeth grit, I snipped the bit of skin away, doused the area with hydrogen peroxide while growling like a damn bear myself, and bandaged it, all the while calling myself a weak chicken shit.

A couple pills popped, and I locked myself up for the night, foot propped up and my head tipped back against my headboard of my bed. The ticking stuffed with dry grass got a nice fluffing every morning after I crawled out to face the day but settled too quickly beneath me every night I laid down.

I considered one of those mattresses that came all rolled up, tight as a drum. Even if Jessie didn't have room in the plane itself, I knew bush pilots often strapped bigger items atop the pontoons. Something to consider, anyway. Maybe a canoe, too, for once I healed up, or at least some super water proofing shit to fix the leak in the old man's that hung on the back of the cabin.

A Snickers bar. Sour gummy worms. A case of Coke. Real Italian bread rather than the sour dough biscuits I'd been making with the starter I'd brought along from Canada.

My mouth fucking watered.

Steak and A1 sauce. Baked potato with sour cream—

Snuffling at the front door ripped my thoughts away from the comforts I missed, and I lifted my head, and stared hard at the wooden latch that couldn't be unlocked from the outside.

My ears strained in the silence, adrenaline kicking my heart rate up. A minute or two passed, and the old trapper's vintage tools hanging on the cabin's side shifted, a clank of metal slamming my heart in my chest and making me think Griz pushed them with his nose.

He snuffed a few times and moved off, shifting noises and grunts pulled my gaze around back of the cabin, tracking his noises.

The old owner had covered up an old cave entrance in the hill's side out back, using it as a cache, I supposed, since the twelve or so foot deep area stayed cool regardless of the outside temperature. I'd rebuilt the face, but rather than use a simple wooden latch a smart as fuck bear could figure out, I'd decided on the padlock I'd brought along. No way that fucker was getting into the stores I'd begun to pack away for the winter.

Still.

Groaning, I rolled from the bed, grabbed my rifle, and checked out all the windows, scanning every inch of my property that I could see. In my state, I wasn't about to head outside, gimpy and unable to run. Not that I had anywhere to run to anyway.

"Where the fuck are you, you big bastard?" I muttered in the stillness, appreciative that the sun didn't sink fully during the Alaskan summer.

Shadows still clung to areas of the landscape, an impenetrable darkness I imagined held the beast who watched me with eyes more intelligent than he ought to possess. Hungry. Feral. Hell-bent on tearing into my throat and wrenching me side to side until I shrieked my last.

A shift of movement beyond my outhouse caught my eye, and I stared hard, my pulse pounding like a goddamn bass drum.

He stepped into the open, a mass of muscle and fur, nose lifting to the outhouse door.

"Fucking Griz." I popped open my window and hollered

like a goddamn lunatic, hating the clench of fear in my gut that bastard instilled.

He lifted onto his hind legs and roared back, jowls snarling and dripping drool like he salivated over eating my face off and ripping me limb from limb.

Instinct stumbled me backward, and I bellowed at the pain in my foot.

"I won't be ruled by you, you fucking cunt!" I screamed out, my voice unsteady and pissing me off.

I shoved the rifle through the opened window, curses flying from my lips at my shaking limbs, and attempted to take aim. My shot went way wide, but it shut him the fuck up, and he dropped and rushed into the brush, making racket enough I heard him flee over the heartbeat slamming in my ears.

"Mother fucking cunt!" I hollered, adrenaline coursing like mad through my blood stream. "Get your ass back here and face me like a man!" Heaving as though I'd run a 5k, I watched and waited at the window.

Every inhale ragged.

Limbs shaking.

"Come on you big bastard," I muttered and had to swallow against the tremble in my voice. "Show your ugly fucking mug so I can blast it to hell."

Silence and stillness mocked me.

"Fucking cunt," I spit out as my adrenaline waned, leaving me a shaking mess.

He didn't return.

Eventually my heart rate slowed to normal, and I buttoned up the window—but I didn't let my guard down. I sat on my lone chair in the middle of the cabin, eyes on the front door.

Waiting.

Muttering.

Half mad with lust of a sort I'd never experienced before. I wanted that fucker dead. By my hand. The need to dominate, show myself the bigger predator, the alpha of my land, consumed my thoughts, keeping me rooted in my chair as though I sat in a tree stand, hunting my prey.

Long hours passed, and my foot throbbed, other knee ached, and eyes grew dry and scratchy. Sweat trickled down my back beneath my t-shirt. I stunk like an animal three days dead in the summer heat.

Eventually it grew dark, casting my home, my escape into true night.

Still, I didn't move. Didn't light a lamp but trusted my straining ears to warn me of Griz's return—because he would. Like any predator, he'd feel the instinctual need to conquer once he got over his fear of the sound of gunfire.

Morning came, and with the sun's rise, came the chickadee's tweets from atop my cabin, waiting his daily bit of cracker. The tin I'd brought had gone stale, but I refused to eat them, saving them for my only friend.

He didn't get any that morning, I didn't take my daily river bath, and I used one of the old man's pots to piss and shit in. My foot fucking throbbed, my knee not much better from the inactivity, but I wasn't about to head outdoors where I'd be a sitting duck. I ate cold beans from a can for lunch and chased them with one of peaches in sweet syrup, licking the tin lid and slicing into my tongue with the jagged edge.

Something else to curse and deepen my scowl.

My cabin smelled like shit and old piss, so I shoved my makeshift toilet out the front door that afternoon, leaving it off to the side, and quickly locked myself back in.

Around dinner, I propped a window open, needing fresh air to clear my fuzzy brain and keep me alert.

The sun set, and I sat in my chair, rifle across my knees.

Minutes, hours, ticked by, and exhaustion pulled at me. Every time my eyelids closed, I saw his gaping jowls. Saliva dripping. I jerked my eyes open, cursed, and shifted on my perch. The bed called, but I remained vigilant.

Day two, same shit, different day, and I muttered more than the first, hobbled from window to window, my throbbing foot keeping me awake, my brain beyond exhausted.

Day three without a bath or real sleep left me in a hazed fog, unable to think properly, and I realized toward evening that I burned with fever. I sat on my chair and peeled off my filthy sock. The bandage I should have changed the day before peeled off too damn easy—puss oozed from the ugly wound.

"Stupid fucker." I retrieved my first aid kit from the bin beneath the bed and gave myself a shot of antibiotics before dumping straight alcohol over the entire foot. I barely managed to keep from screaming, and jaw aching, bandaged it back up.

I downed some pain killers—and a sleeping pill. For my body to battle infection, I needed rest. The goddamn bear couldn't get into my cabin locked up the way it was, and I told myself that fact over and over until I believed it enough to crawl atop my grass ticking.

Need to call and add some shit to my supply list.

"Fucking mattress in a box while I'm at it," I stated with a grunt while stretching out for the first time in days.

Within seconds of laying down on my flattened mattress, I passed the fuck out, all thoughts of predator and prey falling silent to dreams of eating a Snickers bar and taking a hot shower.

12
───────

JESSIE

I couldn't afford a goddamn lawyer. Even my CPA suggested the easy fix of changing my DBA name. Well, I wasn't having it. I'd made a promise to my father while his casket had lowered into the ground—that I would see Midnight Sun Charter in operation again, with me in the pilot seat. I wouldn't ever feel complete without it.

The Blackes had been in business since the first Alaskan bush pilots took to the skies, and I wasn't about to give up over one man's childishness over not getting the pussy he wanted. Fucking rich prick realized I couldn't be bought so had to resort to retaliation to make himself feel better.

"Fucking bastard."

I hadn't smiled in two weeks, and the fact the next month's bills arrived, only deepened my scowl. Couldn't a single woman living alone on the edge of the wilderness catch a damn break? Hadn't I proved to fate, to the gods of wind, sun, and rain, that I was a worthy being? That I deserved to be rewarded for my dedication and hard work?

Fucking Cort had everything handed to him from a rich father who'd moved to the Bahamas or some such tropical so-called paradise. He hadn't worked hard one goddamn day in his life. Sprawling log home featured in all those damn cable shows. Private jet and a dozen cars. The most expensive wine and champagne a man could buy.

Sure, his dad had made good investments while younger —everyone in Fairbanks knew how hard he had striven to make the Endsley name stand out—but Cort?

I snorted and took another sip of my morning coffee.

Two weeks had passed since he'd sauntered up to me with those damn papers, and I was no further along in figuring the shit out than I'd been on that day. I only had another six to file my response with the court, or a judge would rule against me.

My fried eggs grew cold in front of me as I stared at them, the perfectly golden toast alongside them not tempting me in the least.

Not knowing what to do, not having anyone to turn to, haunted me as much as Brock. But, unlike with thoughts of him turning me on, the stress ate away at my stomach. I'd lost a couple pounds—all from my tits and not my thighs, of course.

"Shit." I propped my elbows beside my plate and settled my forehead into my hands. "The fuck am I going to do?"

The silence, for once, didn't settle easy with my mind, and I blew out an exhale through my parted lips. If I had more money, I would take the sky and fly free as a bird, but the cost of fuel, even as a write off, was too much for a self-joy ride.

"This fucking sucks," I said, allowing myself one last sentence of pity.

Lips pressing tight, I lifted my head and chin, and picked up my fork. The cold eggs didn't go down all that easy, but I forced my body to accept the nourishment. I would need all my strength for the battle ahead—

My cell rang, and I pushed up to retrieve it from where I'd left it lie while pouring my second cup of coffee.

The number that had called me a half-dozen times the morning I'd been late to meet a new client…

Brock.

My stomach flipped, churning butterflies into action. A quick swallow, and I swiped to answer. "Hello?"

"Jessie?" His voice alone rippled sexual awareness over my skin, and my nipples tightened.

"Brock." I forced a calm tone—professional—even though wetness creamed between my thighs at my name on his lips.

"Damn, it's good to hear another voice," he said gruffly.

"The frontier too much for you?" I asked with bite in my voice over my body's reaction to him.

"Almost was." He paused, and of course my nosiness took over—not that I *truly* cared.

Liar.

"What happened?" I asked rather than say *good* like my bitchy side considered spewing out.

"I was chopping wood last week. Got distracted and ended up almost cleaving my foot in two."

I sat at the table, cold breakfast forgotten, my insides stilling with true concern. "How's the foot?"

"Got infected." My stomach clenched, but he continued before I could respond. "Been taking antibiotics the last couple of days. It's definitely clearing up."

"So, this isn't a call for rescuing from the land that can't be bought?" I told myself I'd been hoping for that very thing. To prove the rich boy wrong in thinking he could handle my Alaska.

"Nope."

Fuck, he sounded smug, and my scowl returned.

"But I was hoping for a supply run out here earlier than October if possible."

Income.

My damn pride needed to take a back seat.

I hesitated just long enough I didn't sound like an eager beaver to get my plane into the sky. Never mind the pang of instant need that pulsed again between my thighs. "I could probably get out there in a week or so."

"The sooner the better. Gonna need to restock my first aid kit." Brock spouted off a few other things—comfort foods which twitched my lips into a smirk—and I grabbed a pen from my junk drawer and one of my bills, flipping it over to make a list. Wasn't long enough to warrant paying a bush pilot's fees in my mind, but whatever. Wasn't my cash he was blowing.

I needed the money and wasn't about to argue his need for a loaf of Italian bread and a case of Coke. Gummy worms and A1 steak sauce.

"I want one of those mattresses in a box things, too."

My pen stilled, still pressed against the envelope to finish writing a fifty-pound bag of russet potatoes.

"Can't handle roughing it in my wilderness?" The words spewed from my inner bitch, smug as he'd sounded minutes earlier.

"It's fucking heaven out here except for the bed box."

"I can't fit a goddamn mattress in my plane," I reminded him, annoyed over his assumption his money could get him whatever the hell he wanted, regardless of where he lived.

"No—it comes all rolled up tight, air vacuumed, and in a box."

A mattress rolled up and in a box. One of my eyebrows

raised and I held in a snort while questioning his brain. Was the bush doing him in? The solitude, the silence?

"Honest to fucking God," he said when I didn't respond. "Look it up online. Pick out the best quality. I don't care how much it is. Send the link to my accountant along with a bill for the rest, and he'll take care of it."

Anger settled in my gut, and I snipped out an agreement, writing down his CPA's information who handled all his finances. Bank accounts—yes plural—investments, and assets.

To be able to trust someone that fully...

I swallowed against the tears stinging my eyes and the jealousy clenching my chest. Brock Charran was so damn rich, he didn't even have to worry about paying his own goddamn bills.

Cort didn't, either.

Teeth clenched, I jotted down the rest of the information he gave me for future deliveries—still wanting that one in October as well—since I realized he wouldn't be tossing in the towel anytime soon.

"I'll be out as soon as everything gets delivered to the hangar," I told him, hating the excitement rushing through me at seeing him all bearded and sporting longer hair. I needed to get out and get laid before flying to his homestead, so I didn't end up attacking him like a voracious sow in need of dick.

The sooner, the better.

I hung up and eyed the bills in the middle of my table. At least I would have funds to get them paid on time. While Brock's money annoyed the hell out of me, reminding me too much of Cort for comfort, I would take advantage of that shit every chance I got.

Maybe I'd drop a few hints of what he might not realize he missed out on his land. A few of the finer things in life he didn't realize he couldn't live without. A brand-new canoe rather than the stuff he'd ordered to fix up Raymond's dad's.

Or, I could talk him into a 4-wheeler to haul logs. Foster's helicopter would allow me the means to carry it out to him…

One thing at a time.

I hopped online and checked out the mattress in a box thing.

"Huh." I peered closer, realizing I needed to keep up with the times. Definitely needed to talk my other clients into needing what I should have already known about, something a lot easier to deliver than a regular mattress.

An hour later, I put a call through to his accountant and got Brock's order sorted out.

Ten days. Only ten fucking days, and I could head out to see him.

My body primed, ready to roll, but the thought of getting laid elsewhere just to take the edge off my longing for Mr. Rich Man, turned my stomach. No dick, no mouth, no hands would compare to the memory of his.

"Damn him."

Feeding off my pissiness, I called up my own CPA and told him I decided to tell Cort he could go fuck himself. He agreed after a little persuasion on my part—mostly reminding him of his friendship with my father—to help me with the written response.

I couldn't put in the "Fuck you" I would have preferred, but at least I wasn't laying down for Cort to fuck or walk all over.

Hell would freeze first.

13

BROCK

I hadn't realized how much I truly missed another voice until hearing Jessie over the phone. Husky and sexy, hell, even the pissy, short responses stiffened my dick.

But my need to prove myself to her beat out the need to jerk off, so I focused on healing up.

Upon realizing who I was all those weeks ago, she'd muttered I wasn't fit for her wilderness, and her claiming her land couldn't be bought…

As the smartest living being in my wilderness, I ought to dominate. Fear had become my weakness, and Griz fed it like a spring, cold and biting from the dark recesses beneath the earth's surface.

He'd brought out a vulnerability in me I hated. A constitution of the mind I refused to accept as permanent. Fear—and I refused to be a chickenshit again.

Although I still hobbled a bit, my foot felt ten times better after a week or so, fit enough to end my fight with the beast riding my mind and keeping me on edge. I would face my fear and conquer him—or end the life I'd yet to find my self-worth in.

"Show time, you hairy bastard."

Rifle in hand, pack on my back with a few essentials, I stepped out into the bright sunlight and lifted my face to soak in its heat, its fire, its life-giving force. The ultimate adrenaline rush swam through my veins, and I greedily gulped down the fresh mountain air, the scent of pine and soil, remembering the man I had been before the accident.

I opened my eyes and focused on the path ahead of me, determination simmering under my skin and energizing my limbs.

My little chickadee chirped at me, but I left him behind, the instinct to *live* fueling my sure steps. I trekked toward the hills behind my cabin, bracing for war, every step loosening the tightness my bum leg had taken on from being shut up so damn long. Rather than freak out over my hypersensitivity to every damn rustle of leaves or snap of a twig, I funneled it into readiness. Mind over matter. Forced my muscles to relax, but ready to spring. Eyes alert. Ears straining.

I'd survived in Seclusion with a hell of a lot less.

I can do this.

I eased my hold on my rifle, breathing deeply, counting on my inhales, and slowing my exhales as I climbed.

Griz would not beat me. I'd faced many dangers in my life, and the damn animal had ruled over my body long enough. I would prove myself fit for Jessie's wilderness. I would prove myself the dominant species, the ruler of my land. The goddamn alpha in our small part of Alaska.

Pebbles shifted and slid beneath me as I pushed upward, and my foot began to ache. The thought I ought to turn around didn't even enter my mind as I took a breather and studied the lay of the land around me. I'd gone two miles without catching sight of any animal larger than a ground squirrel, and nothing but birds flitted in the brush and thinning trees of the higher hills.

Nothing larger than myself moved in the area, no sixth sense pricked the back of my neck or raised the hairs on my arms.

"He's not up here," I muttered to myself.

I turned a full circle, the altitude I'd gained from climbing offering me a good view of what lay below.

Lazy, leftover smoke curled above my chimney from the fire I'd started hours ago to boil a pot of coffee. A bit of fog still hovered over the river, shifting with the changing breeze.

Griz meandered a good half-mile down river, along its edge.

I lifted my rifle, sighting him through the scope even though too great a distance lay between us for me to attempt a shot. He paused, lifted his nose as though sniffing me out, and started forward once more with a steadier gate as though knowing I didn't linger on the homestead to protect it from his instinctive need to claim and devastate.

If he stayed on course without stopping to fish, he would beat me back to the cabin—even if I ran, which there was no way in hell my foot could handle.

I slung my rifle over my shoulder and started downhill, keeping Griz in sight for as long as possible. A clearing a few hundred yards down into the trees would probably offer me a good view and put me in shooting range of my cabin should his balls take him right up to my front door as he'd done a few times since I'd moved in.

Twenty minutes later, I sucked wind, my quads burning from holding my downhill momentum to a controllable and non-hurting pace. The clearing opened in front of me, a crag of rock and its drop off the perfect spot to sit my ass down.

Knees propped up, I used my binoculars rather than my

rifle to scope the land below in search of him, every flicker of shadow catching my eye. My pulse thrummed from the thrill of the hunt, but I kept my shallow breaths in check, refusing to allow fear to rule my body.

Griz had taken enough from me—my steady nerves I'd never had shattered in such a way, losing sleep like a goddamn chickenshit—my manhood as far as I was concerned. If Jessie ever found out how the wild animal had threatened to loosen my bladder, I'd never hear the end of it.

I refused cravenness further control over my life.

The hard rock beneath me, the clean air ruffling my hair and sweeping over the exposed skin of my face and arms lent me strength, and I sucked it down like the Force actually existed, that the rifle beside me would fit my hand like a light saber.

As though the earth's energy empowered me and my body knew what it needed to do to survive, stillness settled over my muscles and mind. I refused to move other than the slow rise and fall of my chest, and the steady swivel of my head as I studied from left to right and back again. An insect buzzed close by, but I became one with the jutting rock beneath me, unbothered by its presence. Solid. Unyielding to whatever tempest beat against its face.

Instinct morphed me into the hunter of the ultimate preda-tor, and I had one goal in mind—kill the fucking grizzly. Everything I'd studied on the massive brown bears ran through my mind, from reading their body language to the chances of taking them down efficiently.

He stepped from the brush alongside my cabin into the open.

My heart jacked up its pace as I set aside my binoculars and picked up my rifle to sight in on him. Taking into consideration my higher altitude, I adjusted my aim for a heart/lung shot.

"Hold still you hairy bastard," I whispered into the wind, and as if he heard me, Griz stopped and lifted his nose as though scenting me on that downward breeze ruffling my hair.

We stared at one another through my scope.

Silent.

A slow exhale, breath held, and I squeezed the trigger, even though his nearest foreleg wasn't fully forward.

Griz flinched and spun, running his massive form back from the way he'd come, the crash of brush around him reaching me through the clean mountain air.

"Goddamnit!" I hollered, unable to squeeze off the next bullet I'd chambered.

I sat and waited, watching through my scope to see if I could catch a glimpse of him hurrying back up the hills toward wherever his den lay. My pulse slowed as time passed and stillness ruled around me. I'd seen sign of Griz all along my hike up into the mountains, so if he'd planned on heading home—if he wasn't bleeding out somewhere between me and my cabin—I thought for sure he'd pass my way.

He'd had plenty of time and never showed, so I headed down toward the river and home, rifle still in hand, hoping like hell the shot I'd made had been fatal. I got to the clearing around my cabin, every cell in my body wound tight, adrenaline back to pumping and blocking the pain receptors connected to my foot. An extra rush swept over me at the bit of blood splattered across the ground where he'd stood.

"Gotcha," I whispered, scanning the brush he'd taken to.

Slow, measured steps and glances at the ground while stalking forward, every dark red blob alongside scattered pebbles from his flight, fed my confidence. Following the broken path he'd created in his rush through the stand of brush came easy, but the blood dwindled, leaving me on nothing more than a game trail through the trees south of my cabin. Old piles of scat were the only evidence he'd passed that way before.

"Fuck." I crept toward a massive, downed pine, it's knot of roots upturned. The dead, still air denied my senses anything other than the scent of crushed pine needles, rich soil, and decaying wood.

Where are you, you bastard?

As though he'd heard my thought, he rose like a phantom from the hollow that had given the pine life, as silent as the woods around him—and bigger than I'd imagined.

I stumbled back two steps, my mouth dry, my breath seized.

Drool dripped from his jowls as he cracked them open, bellowing a roar that rumbled straight through me.

A scream erupted from my chest, clashing with his terrifying rumble. I held my rifle in front of me without taking time to aim—and shot from the hip.

A tuft of fur and blood erupted from his chest as the gun kicked in my arms, and the tone of his bellow became an outcry of pain.

He swung backward from the force of the bullet.

Dropped onto all fours.

I chambered another round and lifted my rifle to my shoulder, every muscle in my body tensed to snap like brittle twigs.

He spun, his jowls expanded wide enough to encompass my head, and a deafening roar once more filled my ears. Ears laid back, his body tensed to spring with instinctual need to protect himself from a lesser predator whose mind raced.

Skull will glance the bullet away. Eyes no more a target

than a postage stamp. Straight on chest wouldn't drop him with one shot.

I only had one choice. One chance.

I aimed at his shoulder blade and squeezed the trigger.

My bullet ripped through his shoulder and dropped him, the thunder of his voice cutting off in a pained whine.

Without the use of one leg, he couldn't walk, couldn't rush at me.

Calm swept over my mind.

Rifle still tight against my shoulder, I took a few steps forward, pulse pounding, as he scrambled at the ground, desperate yet unable to get his fourth leg beneath him.

"Die you mother-fucker."

I put my fourth bullet in his ear.

He went silent, body still.

My raged breath echoed with the rifle's bark in my ear as I kept him in my sights, hands holding my gun steady. Seconds passed, the rush of adrenaline beginning its downfall.

The shakes began.

I realized sweat trickled down my back. My armpits stank.

The rifle's weight became too much, and my arms sank to my waist, a heavy exhale leaving my lungs as I stared at the ruthless beast I'd reduced to an unmoving mass of fur, bone, and flesh.

Dead. As a fucking door nail.

He'd thought to take what was mine—and failed.

Lifting my face to the dappled sunlight overhead, I let out an animalistic roar to rival his, an alpha's claiming of his territory.

Putting aside my rifle, I pulled my knife and moved in, ready to claim the skin that would keep me warm in the winter to come. The first cut coated my hands in red, and I streaked three fingers beneath my eyes and into my beard, coloring my face with the fucker's life's blood.

His innards spilled out around me, and I stared at the hunk of flesh in my hand—his still heart. Elation rose inside me, and I ripped my teeth into the muscle, the coppery tang on my tongue more fulfilling than any domesticated beef.

I'd taken control of my emotions. Given in to my instincts to pursue the being that had nearly wrecked me—and I'd conquered him.

Wild in heart with a feral mind born of solitude, I chewed and swallowed his flesh with a grin on my face.

An inkling of calm pleasure swept over me, and I set to work taking my trophy.

14

JESSIE

The first time I'd taken control of Dad's plane, my palms hadn't sweated, but flying out to see the man I was determined to hate, had my forehead and between my breasts beaded with moisture.

A little over a half hour of pure torture on my libido as my brain fought my body's wants.

Drop off his shit and get the hell outta there.

My heart raced when his cabin came into view, and I flew in low over the river straight toward his home as though I wished fate intended us to crash into one another once more. A sense of impending tragedy shivered down my spine, raising the hairs on my arms, and I lifted away from the river, buzzed his clearing, and caught sight of him at the brush's edge—shirtless and covered in blood.

"Oh, God." My hands shook, concern over the amount of red smeared over his torso keeping my heart in my throat as I landed upriver and made my way toward the ramp.

He dropped his knife at the river's edge, stalked a few feet into the current, and dove beneath the surface.

Needing to focus, I tore my stare off where he'd gone

under, pulled my Beaver onto the ramp, and shut my baby down, hopping out of the door the second I could safely do so. Brock hadn't surfaced—or he'd dove back down.

I hurried to tie up the pontoons before hopping onto land and spinning back around to scan the river.

Brock's dark head broke the water a few feet beyond my plane, and two strokes of his arms later, he stood in shallow water, his pants hanging low on his hips, stubborn streaks of red still lining his upper body—but no trace of a wound.

"Brock?" I called to him, shaking like a goddamn flag left out on its pole in a blizzard, my fists clenched so tightly my fingernails dug into my palms.

He stalked forward like a prowling lion, no trace of a limp, bulging shoulders hunched, bearded chin lowered. Eyes dark as coal peered at me beneath his furrowed brow, and my heart seized inside my chest as he neared land, river water splashing away from his boots.

Animal.

Feral.

He'd lost his goddamn mind, and I stood frozen in his sights.

Unable to move. Every inch of my skin ready to combust. Wetness pooled to soak my panties.

"Jessie," he breathed my name—a trace of humanity flickering in his gaze.

One last stride, and he grasped my ponytail and my ass, jerking me against his hard, hot form. My squeak cut off by the claiming of his mouth, his hungry lips and tongue seeming hellbent on owning. He tasted of wildness and the forest, a creature at one with his surroundings.

Addictive and damn explosive on my tongue. Damn my libido, and my lack of concern for my well-being. I couldn't get enough.

"Jessie," he groaned against my mouth and lifted me, settling my aching core against the hard length jutting between his thighs.

All thought of concern for *his* wellbeing fled as he grasped my ass in a death grip, rubbed against me, grinding his hips, his cock against my clit. Whimpering, I clutched at his hair, chasing the release I knew he would give even though clothing separated our skin.

He bit my lower lip with a growl, and I detonated, an explosion of stars and fireworks lighting the backs of my eyelids.

"Fuck, Jessie." He swallowed my cries, his tongue lashing, swallowing my breath with a groan. "Fucking need you."

Feral, alright, and barely holding onto sanity while settling me to my feet. He yanked my jeans clear to my ankles without taking time to unbutton them first, leaving a sting along my outer thighs.

One of my boots went flying, and he jerked my jeans off one ankle before standing to take grasp my face and take my mouth once more.

I grappled with the clasp of his pants, panting with the same desperation. Primal need to take, to be taken ruled my senses, and I craved to be beneath him, his skin on mine, his mouth, his branding touch.

"Brock," I managed to plead, and he shoved two fingers inside my dripping core, his other hand dropping to make short work of the clasp I couldn't release keeping me from his cock.

He stroked my inner walls with roughened fingers, his dark eyes filled with fire, untamed need as he pulled back enough to see my face. A deep groan rumbled his chest as I closed my hand around the steel-like length he released.

Heavy breaths passed between us as we stroked each

other, our gazes locked—blue to brown, sky to earth. Stillness settled over me, and I lost myself in the darkness within his eyes, the confidence in his touch. Something within him called to me, making my spirit want to soar beyond the clouds, beyond anything I'd felt in my life.

"What are you doing to me?" I heard myself whisper.

"Need." He yanked me up in his arms, pulling my grip loose from his leaking length, and I settled my legs around his waist as his fingers dug into my ass cheeks.

"Bro—"

He slammed me downward, stealing my breath and shoving every inch of his huge cock deep inside my body. His mouth claimed the rushed exhale leaving my chest, and I clutched at his shoulders as he pounded into me onto him over and over again, grunting with every punch against my cervix.

Holy hell.

I got he'd been lonely, but the man fucked me like an animal, his arms banding around me as though instinct demanded he dominate and conquer. The bitch in me demanded I fight back, make him earn what he wanted—but my body refused.

I relaxed in his tight hold, gave in to my own need, the deepest longing inside me to be taken, owned by a man. Giving up my need for control came easy as he filled me, held me, and fucked me like he couldn't go deep enough, like he wanted to lose himself in my body.

A second climax rose unexpectedly, my pussy walls grasping as I moaned my releasing, coaxing him to join me.

He came with a roar against my neck, his cock impossibly swollen and hot against my womb, his arms stealing my breath with every spurt of his cum.

"Brock," I squeaked the second he quieted, and he loosened his hold but kept me in his arms that had taken on strength and more muscles in the weeks he'd been out in the bush. I clutched at his waist with my legs and threaded my fingers up through his long hair, pulling his face away from me. "Brock?"

The frown had smoothed from his forehead as he met my stare, eyes still unsettled, not fully sane, I feared.

"What happened?" I whispered, not wanting to rouse the wildness lurking in his eyes even though I wouldn't mind another round with the still-hard cock I rested on. "Whose blood was all over you?"

"Griz." He grunted his reply, a glint flashing through his eyes. "Killed the fucker."

"Bear?"

"Mmm." Brock's gaze fell to my lips.

"Are you okay?"

He nodded, lifting his gaze to pierce mine. "But you're not."

I swallowed against the sudden clog in my throat. Did he see the stress lines around my eyes? The bags beneath from sleepless nights? Had he noticed the weight I'd lost in my breasts?

A thundercloud filled his eyes when I didn't respond. "I took without asking. I hurt you."

Clenching my inner walls around his length, I smoothed my fingertips over his scalp, drinking in his groan, trying to soothe his misjudged concern. "I willingly gave—and you didn't hurt me."

"Too rough," he argued, his voice gruff as he lifted me off him, leaving me so damn empty my eyes stung.

Cum gushed from my pussy, and I cupped my hand beneath my thighs, tight against my body to keep from spilling all over my jeans still wrapped around one ankle.

Cock wet and dripping, soaked pants hanging from his hips, Brock knelt and rid me of my other boot and jeans. He swept me up into his arms and carried me like a bride into the river, settling me on my feet once the water crested his knees.

The cold current rippled along my thighs, and I released my hold on my pussy, dipping down into the water to clean myself.

"Let me," he said, his hand once more reaching between my legs, using his hand like a washcloth, rubbing my thighs, my labia, beneath the water's surface.

I clutched at his arm, head tipped back to watch his face as he gently dipped a finger inside me, his thumb finding my clit.

"You're so warm. So soft," he murmured, his gaze going to my lips as they parted. "You taste sweet, like vanilla."

You taste like untamed wilderness, and you look even better.

His languid strokes enticed my inner walls to slicken for more, but he pulled back, his brow furrowing. "Sorry. I meant to clean you not—"

I shushed him with a finger to the soft cushion of his lips, loving the feel of his beard on my palm.

He nodded and let me go, and I followed him to shore, both of us silent.

Not bothering to pull on my arousal-soaked panties, I shoved them in my jean's back pocket once I got them yanked up over my wet legs.

Brock stood dripping, staring at me the entire time, intently enough my face heated. Had he lost all sense of propriety and manners? He'd only been in the bush for a few weeks—

"You're beautiful," he murmured as I pulled on my boot.

And you're fucking hot as hell.

I bit my tongue to keep from admitting his insanely cut upper body, wild hair, and scruffy beard turned me on like no man ever had. Once finished, I stood and moved around him, tossing a quick glance over my shoulder to find his gaze on my ass.

"Want a Coke?"

He jerked his focus up and strode after me, and I let out a chuckle, relieved yet hating he'd taken the bait to lure his mind to other things.

"Do you have to leave right away?" Brock asked while setting his boxed mattress onto the riverbank.

I'd carried the final box of supplies behind him but hesitated from setting it down atop the others we'd unloaded from the back of my plane. "I'd like to see your cabin," I admitted, telling myself I only wanted to see how poorly he managed out in the back country of my Alaska.

His grin, the flash of white teeth, and the light in his eyes hit me square in the damn chest, hardening my nipples. The first I'd seen since arriving, the most human-like expression on his face. "Come on up," he said, grabbed his boxed bed, and strode toward his home. Muscles bulged along his shoulders, every step he took rippling those along his spine. His round ass watered my mouth, and my pussy spasmed with need again.

Calm your tits, woman.

I tore my attention off his fine as fuck form, taking in the homestead he'd made his own.

The raised beds Raymond's father had made out of logs and enclosed with cattle panels I'd flown in a few years earlier still stood, every one of them covered in green and thriving. Brock had been busy splitting and stacking wood, the shed beyond the cabin nearly filled to the slanted roof.

A massive, fresh pelt lay staked out on the cabin's other side, pulling me up short.

Fucking hell.

"Was that your griz?" I asked the obvious, unable to keep the surprise from my voice.

"Was," Brock said without turning.

I took in its size again. A damn monster—he must have stood well over eight feet on his hind legs.

"How'd you do it?" I asked, hurrying to catch up as Brock unlatched his cabin's door.

"Took out his shoulder, then stepped up and put a bullet in his ear."

Stepped up... "How far away was he?"

"Fifteen feet maybe?"

My eyebrows shot up, and I tightened my hold on the box as it began to slip from my hold. Fifteen fucking feet. "Was he charging?"

"Ears laid back like he was about to, but I got the shot off before he sprang toward me."

Well, shit. I had to give Brock credit—he knew more about my land than I ever would have guessed.

Somewhat in awe and hating that fact, I stepped into the cabin behind him, the scent of woodsmoke and man rolling over me. Filling my lungs worsened my want for his cock again, and I squeezed my thighs together while setting the box on his small table. One chair. A full-sized bed box with its ticking he'd told me about over the phone. One pillow.

The rest of his home sat tidy and organized, stacks of canned goods and other boxed foods in neat order on the shelves above his table he'd shoved against one wall.

"The high of the hunt, the kill, still rode me," Brock said, thumping his box onto the floor and turning to face me. "It's why I took you so hard. I'm sorry."

Concern filled his eyes, erasing all trace of the animalistic nature he'd portrayed since I'd arrived.

"Did the release help?" I asked, my damn pride needing to know if I'd given him what he'd needed.

He let out a heavy exhale. "Yes." It seemed he wanted to say more but glanced at the box I'd sat on the table instead. "Will you stay for supper?"

Considering I had nothing to go home to but stress and dread over what summons to court might be awaiting me at the post office, I found myself nodding. "Let me help you get the supplies up from the river, then we can see about some food."

I followed him back down the path and asked him to tell me about his hunt that morning. He gave me all the details, from stepping out into the bright morning sun, to climbing up into the hills, to sitting on a crag and letting fly with the first bullet that had merely wounded and angered the grizzly. To hear how the bear had risen to his hind legs, such a short distance away from him, raced my heart, Brock's words of the bullet ripping into its chest from a hip shot that didn't kill…

"You're lucky to be alive," I told him some time later while helping to unpack the goods I'd brought for him— including new sheets for his mattress that still sat boxed and leaning against the wooden frame he'd been sleeping on.

"I almost shit my pants," he admitted quietly.

I snorted. "What man wouldn't?"

His shoulders relaxed, and I wondered if he'd feared my response to his confession of what some would call weakness. "A rich city boy you thought was unfit for your wilderness."

"Thought," I repeated. "Past tense. You're doing well out here, Brock. You should be proud of yourself."

His beard twitched as though my words, my stamp of approval, pleased him. "Want to help me with this bed?"

I hopped up and helped him lug the old ticking outside.

The foam mattress he'd ordered came vacuum-sealed and rolled just like promised—and the damn thing seemed to swell with life once freed from its packing.

"That's awesome," I said with a laugh, grabbing one end to help him lift it onto the bed frame.

"Gonna feel even better," he said, checking out his new mattress, hands on his hips.

I eyed the dried blood still crusting parts of his upper body. "Why don't you go take a bath in the river like you said you needed while I make up your bed."

He scratched his chest while turning toward me, flaking off a bit of browned blood in the process. "I stink."

"You kinda do." I bit back my smirk, not about to admit that his musk didn't bother me in the least. Sick woman turned on by a man's sweat...

Without another word, he grabbed a bar of soap and folded pair of pants off a shelf, turned, and strode outside, leaving me alone in his home.

Lower lip between my teeth, I poked around the notebooks he kept stacked on the bed stand, wishing I had more time to dive into the journal he'd been keeping about his time in solitude. I expected he wouldn't waste any time getting back to me, so I left the notebooks lay and made his bed as promised.

15

BROCK

J essie looked better than I'd remembered. Tasted twice as sweet. Her pussy more glove-like and silken than I'd remembered while jerking off almost every damn night since our first time together back in that podunk town. Holding her, fucking her on my aching dick had been nothing short of heaven—and I wanted her again.

She seemed different, definitely hurting in some way, but the woman had ten-foot walls like I did. No strings, we'd agreed on, and I wanted it to stay that way, keeping on in my solitude. Sure as fuck enjoyed her visit, though. She'd be back in October, too.

I hurried to scrub my body and hair, tugging up a clean set of pants I'd line dried the week before. Not the most comfortable things, but I couldn't exactly walk around naked like I'd done on occasion while alone.

"Is that rich asshole bothering you again?" I asked her after we'd eaten a couple of fresh bear steaks slathered in A1 and potatoes I'd fried up in cast iron skillets. We sat on my small stoop, barely big enough for two.

Jessie scanned down over the river, her knee jumping like

it'd done on the night I'd met her, and I bumped her shoulder with mine.

"I've got good ears, vixen, remember? Your eyes and that knee say you need to unload."

Lower lip working like she chewed on it, she finally glanced at me. "He owns the trademark on my family business name and is taking me to court."

A shit ton of back story, I expected, and glanced down at her plane and the Midnight Sun Charter logo painted on its side in shades of blue. "Family?"

"My great grandfather started the business. Dad took it over when I was a baby."

"Where's he now?"

"Dead." Sorrow coated that single word, and she cleared her throat as though fighting off lingering grief—something I knew too fucking well.

"Sorry for your loss," I offered, rather than saying I felt her pain.

"Not your fault." Jessie let out a heavy exhale. "I think that rich asshole after my ass was responsible for their accident."

I held my silence, letting her decide how much she wanted to spill.

"He hated my father—and mother especially. Not real sure why." She kicked a pebble with the toe of her boot, and it went scuttling across the worn path leading down to the river.

"Must be some nasty history between him and them."

"Must be." Another exhale sagged her shoulders, and she pulled up her knees, draping her arms around them, and finally stilling her stress energy. "And without knowing, I'm left floundering, having to ward off his advances until he gets the damn memo. His retaliation is ending my dream to rebuild what Dad lost."

Lost. Definitely back story, but I wasn't going to pry. She'd spilled more than I'd expected her to.

"So anyway." She flashed me a fake-ass smile. "That's my stressor these days, but it's just a blip on my life's radar. I'll rise above whatever ashes remain and keep flying the free skies."

"You will," I agreed without hesitation. If anyone could, the stubborn, driven vixen would.

"Tit for tat, rich boy. Tell me why you're out here hiding in the wilderness."

"Not hiding. Decompressing and enjoying the peace and quiet."

"Not so quiet right now."

"You're a welcome reprieve," I said with a chuckle. "I'll enjoy the silence again once you're gone."

Fire shot from her eyes, twitching my dick. "Guess I'll get going, then."

The comment I wasn't sure I truly meant—or claimed with snark—had snuck through a crack in her exterior, if her snippy tone was any indication, and I grabbed her before she could stand, pulling a squeak from her lips while tugging her onto my lap.

"Don't go just yet."

"Why not?" she snapped, ice in her eyes, tension in her body that felt too damn good under my hands.

"Cuz I'm not done with you."

"Well, I'm done with you." She made no move to escape, but she didn't melt against me, either.

I wrapped her ponytail around my fist and tipped her head back, her glare narrowing as I tugged. "Liar."

She opened her lips to argue, but I shut her down with

mine, groaning at the sweetness of her soft, wet mouth. Her body went pliant against me, her whimper swelling my dick for another round.

"Stay with me tonight," I whispered, pulling back enough to find warmth and arousal filled her eyes.

She studied my face long enough I felt sure she'd decline. "Just the one night," she finally said, her tone firm.

"One night."

"No strings."

"No strings." Yeah, I liked the hell outta her, her sass, her spunk and drive, but I loved my land. My solitude. The silence and lack of judgment.

"You just want to try out that new mattress," she said, the corner of her lip twitching up.

"Damn right." I grinned and stood, keeping her in my arms.

Jessie wrapped hers around my neck, fingers playing with the curling hair at my nape. "Gonna let me take you how I want you?"

"Told you before, woman, you can ride my dick anyway you like. Won't hear any complaints from me."

"Let's go mess up those new sheets." Her husky purr and nip on my ear lobe leaked pre-cum from my aching length.

"I need to do laundry tomorrow anyway."

———

Jessie rode me, alright, and passed the fuck out long before true darkness took over the sky outside my window. Light snores passed her parted lips, and I stayed on my side, staring at her while she slept. Creep from hell, but I wanted every line on her face, the fall of her hair, the gentle twitches of her closed eyelids imprinted in my head for the months ahead.

Wasn't real sure why I felt I needed to drink my fill, but I did.

I hadn't gotten any more of her family and that asshole's shit from her, but I'd heard enough to be concerned. I also expected she didn't have the funds for a lawyer to fight for her in court. She'd only just begun to rebuild her family's company, so there was no way in hell she rolled in the dough —especially considering the state of that old truck she drove.

But I could help.

She wouldn't let me—no doubt about it, so I told myself she didn't need to know.

That thought rolled me off my new mattress which was comfortable as fuck, and I snuck out into the twilight, sat phone in hand. It was only around nine on the east coast, and I was good enough friends with my financial adviser to call him all hours of the day. He picked up, and within a half hour, I helped eased her burdens. More than enough to cover lawyer and court fees also landed in her bank account since I had access to set up payment for my supplies. Anonymous, untraceable, that time, however, the money would help her continue in her dream to rebuild her family's company. Because I had money to spare with no immediate family in need, why the fuck not? Jessie, the small fish, seemed like good people, and the thought of her dreams going down the drain like mine had didn't sit well in my gut.

Besides, I wanted her to be my link to civilization. I wanted to see her sassy smirk, her cold eyes go warm with a tint of green every chance I got. She needed a plane for that to happen—so *I* would make it happen.

I slid beneath the sheets a few minutes later, and Jessie rolled into me with a sigh, her limbs tangling with mine. "Jessie?" I whispered, checking to see if I'd woken her and could bury my dick inside her hot body again.

She let out a small snore, and I grinned, gathering her up against my chest a little tighter, loving the soft cushion of her tits between us. Face buried in her sweet-smelling hair, I closed my eyes and breathed the scent of vanilla into my lungs. I would wake her in the morning, eat her, fuck her, then send her off sated and smiling.

No nightmares of grizzlies came to wake me with a start, no images of fangs, claws, and roars to shiver my skin with goosebumps. I slept like a goddamn baby for the first time in … since I'd spent the night with her the first time around.

The roar of an engine woke me from a deep, dreamless sleep, and I realized I wouldn't get the opportunity to send the little vixen away how I'd intended.

Jessie had slipped out of my bed and out the door, same as I'd done to her at the hotel.

I hurried outside, bare-assed naked, cursing, and scowling. Hands on hips, I stood on my stoop as her Beaver bobbed down river, propeller spinning like mad to take her away from me.

She lifted into the sky with ease, a bank tilting her wings, heading back toward civilization.

No fly by. No goodbye.

But we hadn't agreed to anything more.

Rubbing at the strange ache in my chest, I went back inside rather than go dive into the river for my morning bath. I wanted to keep the scent of her on my skin for as long as possible.

16

JESSIE

I panicked.

The scent of Brock had filled my lungs, woke the hunger between my thighs, and I had opened my eyes to find his peaceful face mere inches from mine. We shared a pillow. Shared our breaths. But he'd stolen the blankets.

In that moment, I'd been too heated, too suddenly strung out to be anything but flaming hot from the inside out.

Luckily, I'd managed to slide out of bed without waking him.

A damn chickadee atop the stoop's overhang chirped a chipper hello when I stepped outside. I cursed him under my breath while quietly clicking the door shut behind me.

He flitted after me as I hurried to my plane, my heart in my throat, my hands shaking.

I should have done the usual pre-flight check but cut it short in my need to get the hell away from the man who made me feel things I didn't want. The need to submit, the desire to let a man care for me, the want of him—his scent, his touch, his gaze on whether it be feral or human, lust or longing.

"The fuck is wrong with me?" I blinked wetness from my eyes and focused on the eastern horizon.

I hadn't looked back, hadn't glanced at his cabin as my Beaver had come to life. The longing to do so had me biting my lip against the thickness, the tears clogging my throat as I flew away, leaving him behind, not even checking to see if he watched or cared.

Wind buffeted my plane same as thoughts did to my head. My heart had melted at Brock's touch, at the comfort I'd felt when waking in his strong arms. For those five or so minutes I'd watched him sleep, no stress attempted to fracture my brain. The ache of loss in my chest soothed by his presence. My heart felt he'd offered safety, but my head… I needed to stay in control to stay safe.

Relying on someone was a mistake I refused to make. The one I'd love the most had let me down in his weakness—how could I trust another?

"I don't hold any bitterness in my heart, Dad. I'll fix your mistake. Make the right decisions. I promise." I choked on my words and swiped tears from my cheeks.

With the shit waiting for me at home, I knew I'd be too busy, too stressed out, to think. Work had been my shield for many years, my greatest strength. I wouldn't allow the cracks I felt shifting inside me to hinder my strides toward attaining my goals. Embarrassment over telling Brock the little bit I'd spilled shifted me on my seat. I didn't share weakness with anyone. Speaking that shit out loud always seemed to make it more real.

"I'm strong enough on my own," I told the atmosphere, telling fate how things would go. "I will stand on my own two feet. I will see things right by my dad."

Fate laughed back.

A few hours later, I sorted through my mail. No court

summons, but a handful of bills waited for me. I got online to check how many pennies I had in my bank account, and five-hundred thousand stared back at me.

"The fuck?" Laughing at the joke, I refreshed my browser, got kicked out of my banking app, and logged back in.

The money still showed.

Forehead skin bunching up in a deep dent, I called my bank and let them know they'd accidentally made a deposit into the wrong account.

Nope.

The wired transfer had been intentional, verified twice, and made by an anonymous donor. I couldn't get any more information than that.

Hand numb, I hung up and stared at my computer screen, baffled for all of three or more seconds.

"Fucking Cort." My scowl returned. He thought he could *buy* his way into my pants since I hadn't bent to his threat of lawsuit tactic? "Motherfucker."

I grabbed a pen and my check book without further thought. The asshole couldn't buy me, but that didn't mean I wouldn't look a gift horse in the mouth. I paid off everything. *Everything.* And I hired myself a lawyer for the fight ahead—I wondered why Cort didn't consider that before attempting his bribe.

"Stupid fuck."

Flicking the red flag on my mailbox, I grinned down the dirt lane leading to my tiny town. Fate had given me two extra feet to stand on—hell, more like five-hundred thousand more feet—and I planned to use them to my benefit to finish what I'd set out to complete.

————

Cort showed up at Foster's the next week as cold rain muddied the lot. Actually looking forward to the exchange, I sat back in the office chair and waited, feeling more than a bit smug over finding my debt gone online earlier that morning. I'd caught a northerly wind to glide on, and nothing would send me down.

"You're making a mistake." His cold eyes flashed, and I raised an eyebrow in question. "If you think for one second I'll drop this lawsuit," he continued, "you've got another thing coming."

"Think."

He blinked at my bland tone, his brow furrowing deeper. "What?"

"Think," I repeated, biting back my smirk. "You've got another *think* coming."

"What the fuck ever, Jessie," he snipped his words. "I offered to make all this go away. I offered you the world most women would leave their husbands for."

"World?" I snorted.

"And now you're forcing me to take when you could have freely given. We could have been something together." That unhinged look took over his face, softening his features and easing the tension in his shoulders.

I should have been eased by his relaxed stance, but my stomach twisted, and the hair rose on my nape.

"You're so much like him." Cort's gaze flicked over my face with a tenderness that churned my breakfast with sour bile, his focus going hazy like he disappeared in his mind.

"It's time for you to leave," I told him, my voice shaking as I straightened in my chair.

He blinked and stepped back as though I'd slapped him. "You—you're just like him." Cort sounded like a whiny little bitch, but he straightened, the coldness taking over his face like he had two personalities sharing his brain. "Deny me and you'll wish you'd never been born."

Ice slid through my veins, freezing me through. "Get. Out."

"You're dead to me." Cort spit on the floor.

"I was never anything to you before," I reminded him coldly although my insides quaked.

"Fuck you."

"I'll pass, thanks."

"You'll be sorry you denied me, Jessie."

Staring, chin lifted, I grinned in response to his threat. My fingers itched to pull Foster's sawed-off shotgun from its hiding place beneath the desk, but I never acted on impulse. His family would fry me.

No, Cort had burned himself by giving me that money. The rich prick had dug his own grave, and I would spit on it once my lawyer he paid for helped me take him down.

"You'll be sorry." He muttered a few curses while spinning and slamming out the door, but I ignored those insults, too. Yes, I was a stubborn ass like my dad, and I took pride in that fact.

My adrenaline high crashed, and the inner tremors took over my limbs. I wrapped my arms around my center and offered what comfort I could. Longing for Brock's arms slammed into me like a gale force, catching my breath.

My own two feet, I reminded myself, lifting my chin. *My own.*

17

BROCK

D ays passed. Weeks passed.

I found myself returning to myself, the fear gone, a sense of humanity I'd lost in killing Griz slowly settling back inside my head.

His skin eventually made its way into the cabin, scraped, tanned, and softened, and sat at the end of my bed for when cold weather truly hit. Enough bear jerky lay stored up for the months ahead, and I'd even gone all old-school whittle-man on the bones, making utensils and a bear claw necklace.

Four bear 'hams' hung in in the back of my cache where it stayed cool enough the meat wouldn't turn rancid. I had a few jars of bear lard rendered down and had dined on ribs I'd soaked and smoked over an open fire for days on end.

A sense of satisfaction I'd never experienced before settled over me every time I glanced at the fur on my bed, though. A bed that had felt too empty since Jessie had snuck out. It's like that taste of woman, that sharing of space where a man lay most vulnerable, had instilled an instinctive hunger in me.

I craved her, and not just the sex.

Her scent, her husky voice.

My little chickadee hung out with me every morning while I drank black coffee on the stoop while thinking of her, his tweets and chirps enticing me to carry on with a one-sided conversation like my mom did with her tiny lap dog.

After Jessie's taking off, it was Chick's presence, his want for me, that helped calm the beast I sometimes felt rise up inside me. He also hung nearby when I worked in the garden or hauled logs over my shoulders back to the cabin to cut and split.

I eventually put my faith in him to alert me to danger—twice to a smaller black bear who took an interest in my homestead. The young bear had scared the shit out of me the first time Chick flitted off while I'd bathed.

The bear came lumbering along through the brush while I tread water, neck-deep in the river. He sniffed at my dirty clothes, pawing them a bit. Not Griz, but still.

I waited, and he eventually moved off down river. While darkness inside me itched my feet to hunt, kill, and prove my dominance, I reasoned with myself—I had no freezer. No way to preserve another pile of bear meat that wouldn't go bad before I could consume it. I wouldn't waste.

The third time Chick alerted me to danger came as I split wood, making enough racket to keep animals away. My neck hairs stood on end as he lifted off into the sky with his usual danger-alerting chitters.

A "Hello the cabin!" rang out, jerking me around.

Gray-bearded, straggly hair pulled back in a low ponytail, and wearing a vest made of what looked like a wolf pelt, an old man approached. He glanced around my clearing, his stooped shoulders hinting at age, but his sure steps and steady gate telling another story.

Predator.

I straightened, sliding my hand down my axe's shaft to let it rest on the log beside me. "Hello," I called in return, giving him a quick once-over.

He carried a knife on his hip, its pommel worn smooth—probably from use considering his age. Rugged buckskin-like pants, boots that had seen better days, a sack over one shoulder, an old rifle on the other.

His stench drifted downwind as he pulled up a dozen or so feet away from me, wafting past my nose like obnoxious fumes, curling my nose.

"Heard there was a new fella over here," he said, revealing black teeth bracketing holes where ones ought to be.

"Brock Charran," I offered, making no move to greet him properly.

"Shiv Arntz." He sniffed and wiped the back of his hand across his scared nose. "Live over the mountain there." He pointed over his shoulder, and I realized he was the neighbor Jessie had told me about.

"Used to come over and trade with Roy," he continued. "My girl makes berry preserves every year this time. Heard the place got sold off and figured I'd take a little hike to see if you got anythin' to trade."

My hairs still stood an end, an inner sense telling me the man couldn't be trusted. Then again, I'd been in the bush long enough I felt more at one with her than man. "You looking for cash or goods?"

His murky hazel eyes set my teeth on edge as he checked me out from head to toes. "Depends on what you got."

"Cash and grizzly jerky." The two things I had more than enough of.

"Got yerself a griz?" he asked, his gaze flitting down over

me once more like he sized me and my expensive outdoor gear up.

I'd ripped off my t-shirt an hour earlier and knew what he saw. A muscle-packed man more than capable of defending his home. Well on my way to becoming seasoned by the Alaskan summer, I didn't doubt my abilities to take him down if he went all feral on my ass.

The homestead had become my home, and I wasn't about to let some backwoods, filthy man try to swindle or steal from me.

"I did," I finally answered him.

"The good earth provides fer those who care for her," he said, nodding as though approving of me.

The tension eased a bit from my shoulders, but I kept myself on edge, riding the darkness if need called for it.

"Jerky's good." Shiv smacked his lips.

"It's out back." I motioned beyond the cabin.

He nodded and moved in the direction I pointed, watching me side-eye as I pulled my shirt back on over my head.

"Got a woman?" he asked.

"No. Just me out here." I pulled abreast of him but kept far enough away my stomach wouldn't roil from his stench.

"Must get lonely without pussy."

While the observation coming from a buddy would have had my lips twitching, Shiv's words tightened my gut.

"I buried my woman last spring," he continued when I didn't reply, "but her daughter looks after me and the house now. Good girl, that one." He made a moan-like noise in the back of his throat, stirring that darkness inside me.

His daughter, Jessie had said.

"How old?" I asked, unlocking my cache's door and watching him like a hawk in my periphery.

"Fourteen. Old enough to bleed and give me a son, but she ain't conceivin'."

Sick. Fuck. Teeth grit tight, I pulled the door open. "Wait here," I grunted, keeping my eye on him while I took two steps into the cache to grab the first sack of jerky in reach.

I wanted the fucker gone—and tossed him the sack, my muscles coiled to spring and use that knife at his hip to rip his throat open from ear to ear. Sick, perverted pedophile.

"Think my ball sack is too old," he grumbled, switching out my sack for the one he'd brought over his shoulder. "I'll bet you could give her what she wants."

"What?" The word shot past my lips as my scowl locked into place.

"Yer young. Bet a cock full of yer sperm would give us a baby."

Fucking A.

"No," I forced the word out through grit teeth and dug my ragged fingernails into my palms to keep from ending him.

"She's a pretty thing." He held out the sack of preserves he'd brought along which I hesitated to take. "Silky black hair just like her momma. Blue-green eyes like her daddy." Shiv's own hazel eyes peered at me, with a calculated glint that crawled my skin.

"Not interested." I set the sack aside and locked up my stores.

"Tiny little tits, but her pussy is warm and snug—best thing I own."

I nearly gagged and swallowed against the urge to vomit.

"She'd give you her ass, too. Tight puckered hole I make her keep clean as a—"

"Thanks for the preserves," I said, cutting him off and striding back toward my axe, the darkness flexing my fingers to split his fucking head wide open, leave his brains for whatever carnivorous critter needed a full belly.

"Sure I can't change yer mind?" He hurried after me. "She's a good cook—come on over the mountain and spend a few days. Get yer fill of pussy. I don't mind sharing. She'd be happy to have a young thing like you rather than my old cock that she's gotta suck on to make hard—"

I spun and grabbed hold of his neck, the sack in my hand falling to the ground as I reached for the hand he grasped at his knife with.

"I don't fuck little girls," I hissed in his face, ignoring his stench while leaning in close to make my point. "And I sure as fuck won't be donating any sperm. Get the fuck off my property, and if I see you here again uninvited, I'll shoot first and ask questions later. Understood?"

I held his wrist in a bone-crushing grip, easily overpowering his slighter frame.

He licked his lower lip and grinned, flashing his rotted teeth. "Understood." The hint of madness in his eyes promised me he'd be back.

Fucking cunt.

"Leave." I shoved him away from me, and he stumbled a few steps before lifting the bag of jerky.

"Good trade!" he called before turning to hike away.

Good trade, my ass.

I watched him enter the brush before grabbing up my rifle from where I kept it leaning against the woodshed like I always did when splitting. Eventually, I caught sight of him through my scope, tracking his progress through the pass between the two mountains. Temptation to put a bullet in the back of his head warred with the fact he was the girl's provider in a wild land.

"Not my circus," I told myself, finally setting my rifle aside.

Two of the old canning jars of jam had smashed when I'd dropped Shiv's sack, but I dumped the rest of the preserves into the river, scrubbed out the three remaining jars, and chalked up the bad trade as a lesson well learned.

I might be in the wilderness, but there were definitely more than animals I needed to look out for.

18

JESSIE

We had him, my lawyer assured me. While Cort submitted documentation about his owning the trademark on Midnight Sun Charter, he hadn't utilized the company. My dad's plane had been repainted with his own logo in red, doing away with the old blue. None of his adverts, nothing in Endsley Flight Services listed a single word about Midnight Sun.

Yes, the judge was a cousin once removed or some such shit of Cort's, but my lawyer was good friends with Alaska's attorney general. If the judge didn't rule fairly according to the law, he stood a good chance of getting his wrist slapped—or worse. With my lawyer's help, I could assure him of that fact.

The judge considered the papers both my and Cort's lawyer had provided. Ours shows the actual file date of Cort's trademark renewal—one day late. His own lawyer had submitted a document that stated otherwise.

I clasped my hands on my lap, knuckles white, waiting in the heavy silence that fell over the court room. My fingernails dug into my palms as I willed my pulse to slow, to show calm and confidence as my lawyer did beside me.

Clearing his throat, the judge looked up, his gaze on Cort's side of the room. "Regardless of the dates listed on these renewals, you've offered no proof the trademark name is currently in use."

Cort shifted. "But Your Honor—"

"Judgement is for the defendant." The gavel came down with a sharp bang, twitching my body with a wince even as I grinned with relief.

Cort hopped from his chair, letting out a string of curses, and I slouched back in my seat, a heavy exhale leaving my tight throat as he continued to spew shit at me.

The gavel continued to bang as the judge called for order —Cort ended up being escorted out.

An adrenaline crash left me trembling, but I stood along-side my lawyer who gathered his papers. "Thank you."

"My pleasure, Ms. Blacke. And, I'll have your trademark papers filed by the end of the day."

My shaking legs carried me outside, and I pulled on my coat against the cool bite in the October air. The sun felt warmer even though it wasn't high in the sky. The hustle and noise of Fairbanks didn't grate on my nerves as it usually did.

I'd won.

Grinning and thinking about how to celebrate, I unlocked my new truck's door. A premonition shivered over my skin—

"I'm going to end you."

I closed my eyes as Cort's voice killed my high. Spinning, I found him inches from my body, his body trembling, his eyes iced with rage. "Your plan backfired, asshole, and if you don't obey the restraining order my lawyer forced on your cousin, I'll make sure you end up in jail, too."

"Fucking bitch." He backed off, shoulders hunched, and hands fisted at his sides.

"Money can't buy you everything," I tossed out, wanting him to know he wasn't all powerful anymore. But money had definitely helped me defeat him. I yanked open my truck's door, climbed in, and rolled the window down. "Thanks for the gift, by the way. I put it to good use, didn't I?"

I left Cort standing in the lot staring after me, his brow furrowed, hands fisted at his sides.

Stupid asshole.

Laughing, and once again shaking from an adrenaline crash, I headed toward home. Celebrating sounded like one hell of a good idea, but it wasn't just a few drinks I wanted.

Brock.

My body went warm at the thought of him. It'd been almost six weeks since I'd left Brock, and the following morning my schedule promised a delivery to his homestead, including a case of Coke and a box of Snickers bars he'd called two weeks earlier to tack onto his list.

A storm forecasted to hit our area mid-morning, bringing early snow and high winds. Staying put until it cleared would be a smart move, but not once had Dad rescheduled, going back on his word to deliver promised goods. Midnight Sun Charter delivered. Period. I'd told Brock I would be there on October the seventeenth, and nothing would stop. me. If that meant a flight at six in the morning, then so be it.

Even better, flying in an hour before the storm would ensure I'd have to stay out in the bush for a day or two until the weather cleared. Get my fill of Brock and his cock I fantasized about riding again.

Hell, I deserved a break. A vacation. Where better to spend it than on a boxed mattress fucking a man who'd gone without a woman for six weeks?

19

BROCK

I hadn't heard from Jessie, so the second I woke up, my ears strained, waiting for her arrival. Too cold for coffee on my stoop, I stood and fed Chick from my hand while watching the overcast sky, shivering after only a few minutes outside in a sweatshirt.

The cold bit through my pants, reminding me of my old knee injury, something that hadn't bothered me most of the summer since I hardly sat still.

And this is only the beginning.

Chick chirped and pecked at my hand some more. Smirking at my little friend, I realized I would have to feed him through the winter. He'd come to depend on me for his morning meal. I couldn't leave him scrambling through the long winter ahead.

"I'll take care of you, Chick. Don't mind that responsibility."

He chirped again and flitted off into the brush where he'd been fluttering from every morning, and I expected he'd build his home.

Hands on hips, I studied the sky. A kick of cold wind

blasted my face, and a sense of wanting to hunker down in my cabin swept over me. Incoming storm? Or the want of Jessie in my bed to keep me warm?

October seventeenth—delivery day. Would she fly out if a storm approached like the incoming clouds promised? Last I'd spoken with her, she'd said if it stormed, she'd be out once it cleared. But she'd also promised to make my deliver that day.

I'd scrubbed my cabin, cleaned my sheets, and left them hanging to dry inside the cabin the day before since it'd barely got above freezing during the day. I'd fluffed my only pillow earlier that morning, tucked in the clean sheets, and got a pot of bear stew going over the fire all before six a.m.

But would she come?

Come. My dick jolted.

I wanted her in my cabin. In my bed. Coming on my mouth and around my girth, countless times.

Dick aching and lips pursed, I let out a huffed exhale and went back inside for another cup of coffee. Best to keep busy to take my mind off her arrival, my drawn-up nuts, and butterflies running riot in my stomach because of it.

The sky grew darker and the gusting wind smelled like snow as I split the wood I'd cut up the day before, dropping my spirits. She wouldn't make it. Slamming my axe into the final log, I let out a few curses, hating the disappointment aching my chest. While I'd yet to find complete peace in the wilderness, I'd found contentment in the simple life. I'd hoped to be content without pussy, but having tasted Jessie on my own turf, that hope had flown the coop. The thought of having to wait a few extra days pissed me the hell off.

I swiped my forearm across my sweaty brow, and a low whine grew in the distance.

Jerking my head around, I studied the sky, straining to make out Jessie's plane…

There.

A flush of excitement, a rush of adrenaline welled up inside me, stiffening my dick again, and I grinned like a goddamn idiot while putting my axe away under the lean-to. I grabbed the last two pieces of wood I'd split and tossed them atop the pile that would easily see me through the winter.

Time for a goddamn break.

She buzzed over my clearing, and I lifted a hand to wave as a loud bang erupted from the plane.

"Fuck!"

The right wing caught in a sudden gust of wind, jerking the plane toward the ground.

"Jessie!" I screamed and ran, knowing even as the engine cut out and she skimmed the brush she wouldn't make it to the river to land. Memories slammed into me, flashes of lights and beeps. Screams. My hollering for my passengers to hold on…

"Jessie!"

A tree took off one of her Beaver's wings, and the plane spun, the crunch of metal ringing in my ears as my pulse thrummed, adrenaline pumping as fast as my numbed legs took me through the trees.

No explosion.

But silence too fucking heavy settled as quickly as the crash occurred. Curses and prayers rang through my head, faster than my pulse pounded in my ears as I sprinted forward.

Please be okay… Please be okay…

Wind whipped at me as I tore out of the stand of trees south of my property. The plane sat in a mangled mess yards from the river, lying on its side, one wing still pointing to the sky. Smoke—but no fire.

Pushing against vivid memories of my mangled Betsy, I took off again, one small rock twisting my knee enough I grit my teeth from the pain. I could make out Jessie through the front window, head hanging to the side, blood dripping.

"Oh fuck. Fuck, baby, please be okay…" Ignoring my throbbing knee, climbed up onto the crunched cabin, yanking at the door with burning muscles until its bent form squeaked open. "Jessie!" I reached in and gently touched her neck, my damn hands shaking.

Steady pulse.

"Thank fuck." Gentle as I could, I unhooked her and pulled her out of the plane. For the first time since I'd hidden myself out in the bush, I wished to be closer to civilization. Paramedics. Nine-one-one and hospitals. "Got you, vixen. Hold on for me, okay?" My voice shook like the leaves still clinging to trees' branches.

I cradled her in my arms and hurried back the way I'd come the best I could with my throbbing knee, leaving the plane without a backward glance.

"You're going to be okay," I murmured against her forehead, sticky blood clinging to my lips. "I got you."

Holding her tight against my chest, I used my foot to pry open my cabin's door. Ragged breaths ripped from my lungs as my first ever panic attack kicked into high gear. Every muscle in my body tensed like a motherfucker and yet trembled like a newborn calf.

Fucking fear, and ten times worse than what Griz had brought to life inside my craven gut.

"Got you," I murmured, carefully laying her out on my bed before swiping my forearm across my lips to rid them of her blood. I grabbed the battery-operated lantern off my table and held it up to better see her face while using one of my clean shirts to staunch the blood flow from the nasty laceration on her head.

A quick scan down over her body didn't show another trace of red, but I set the lantern above the bed on the small shelf I'd built, and tied a bandage around her head to better stop the seeping wound. I set out cutting off her clothing, careful as fuck to not jostle her more than I already had just in case of internal injuries or broken bones.

In panties and sports bra, she appeared fine. No cuts, no obvious signs of injury.

But she wasn't waking up.

I checked the head injury to find it swelling and cursed under my breath for not having a freezer or ice. Scrubbing a hand down over my face, I considered the cut, too. Not deep enough for stitches, but it definitely needed help. While digging the bin from beneath the bed that held my first aid kit Jessie had restocked earlier that summer, I tossed out a couple of prayers to every god I could think of, including Mother Nature herself who'd sent Jessie's plane down after whatever that bang had been.

A couple of butterflies would do the trick for the cut, but I couldn't do a damn thing about the bump or her not waking up.

Time would tell.

I grabbed my sat phone and returned to her side, powering it up to put through a call to Foster's hangar.

No one answered, so I pulled up the other number I'd saved on that day Jessie had shown up late to bring me out to the homestead.

Endsley Flight Services.

No one answered there, either, and I cursed the fact they didn't man the phones on a Saturday morning. Still cursing in my head, I waited for the answering service to shut the fuck up so I could leave a message after the beep—but they offered an emergency number to call, and I scrambled for my pencil and notebook on the bed stand, quickly jotting it down.

"Cort Endsley," he barked after a few rings.

"Mr. Endsley—this is Brock Charran. I'm a customer of Midnight Sun, and Ms. Blacke crashed her plane near my homestead about an hour ago." My damn voice shook.

"Is she okay?" he asked before I could spew any more information.

"She's banged up a bit and is still out cold. I can't wake her. Any chance you could get a plane or helicopter out here the second this damn storm breaks?"

"Of course. Of course." He sounded out of breath, and I shot off the coordinates for my homestead, giving him Raymond's name. Cort knew the place. "I'll get someone out there as soon as I can," he assured me, "but can you keep me informed about her wellbeing? I've known Jessie for a long time."

"Sure thing." I kept my focus on Jessie, more concerned about her than who Cort might be to my vixen.

My vixen. It sounded right—and fucking felt right.

I hung up a few seconds later and powered my cell off to save the battery, my guts all twisted up, but at least the muscle tremors throughout my body had stopped.

The day passed slow as fuck, and Jessie didn't stir or twitch a goddamn muscle. I prayed. Stoked the fire. Tucked my blankets around her body better. Pulled the bear skin up to her waist. Brushed hair off her forehead. Rubbed my aching knee while sitting and staring at her in silence like a creepy fucker.

My eyes burned as exhaustion set in, and I dimmed the

light and crawled onto the bed beside her, careful to not touch her too-still form.

Lips parted, she breathed quietly and steadily.

"You gonna wake up for me, vixen? I'd sure as fuck love to hear your husky voice right now. See your eyes spit fire at me. Listen to your sass that turns me the fuck on."

Nothing.

Letting out a heavy breath, I settled in for a long night, knowing I wouldn't sleep.

20

BROCK

The storm went from white-out to gray skies and back again for three long days. I managed to get some bear bone broth and water down Jessie's throat, but she still hadn't stirred other than to swallow on reflex. Even her body relieved itself without effort on her part. Thank fuck for the extra towels I kept in a bin beneath my bed.

I forced so many damn liquids down her throat, all but one hung on the line I strung inside the cabin to dry clothes.

My sat phone wouldn't put through calls during the quiet moments I powered it up, so Cort's updates would wait same as I did for her rescue.

How could I watch her be spirited away?

How could I stay on the homestead alone, wondering what the fuck was happening? How she fared? If she woke or stayed in a coma?

A million other questions flitted through my head, like how could I have gotten so attached to a woman I hardly knew? Was I that lonely out in the bush and I just hadn't realized it? But even with her silent and still, that energy connecting us still raged through me.

And giving her a sponge bath on day three?

Fuck.

My dick stiffened hard as hell, but I grit my teeth and washed her body, knowing she was going to throw a goddamn hissy fit when she realized I'd had to wipe between her thighs and ass while she lay unconscious. She'd be embarrassed. Wanting to take off, leaving me behind.

Jessie Blacke wasn't the kind of woman who liked to show weakness, and I expected she would hate me for seeing her in her worst state.

Her nipples pebbled as I washed the slopes of her breast, my breath ragged as fuck while she lay unmoved. Her body responded to my touch—or was it simply the cold?

I tossed another log on the fire and returned to my task, my dick aching to take, the instinct inside me that rode the edge of sanity wanting the same. I'd never known such wicked temptation that swayed the darkness, the animal growing inside me.

She won't know.

"Fucking asshole—you're not touching her." I grit my teeth, washed down over her stubbly-haired legs and feet, taking my time to rub each and every toe.

Still, she didn't twitch.

The wind howled outside, rattling the shutters I'd latched. Darkness lingered in the cabin's corners, untouched by the fire's flickering flames. Embers cracked but didn't soothe me as they usually did.

At least my bum knee had calmed the fuck down, allowing me to move around the cabin without wincing at every step.

I washed my own body down before crawling into the bed beside Jessie, once more on my side to watch her until I passed the fuck out.

With the morning came a break in the storm and clouds, and I stepped outside into wind-blown drifts of light snow over a foot deep in some areas. For the amount of storming it'd done, I'd expected closer to six feet. Guess the wind carried the white shit where it wanted, same as the nor'easters back in New England.

Still no phone service, but at least Jessie's condition hadn't worsened. I realized her body kept her out in order to heal. I just needed to be patient—and continue with my prayers to whoever might hear my mutterings.

I planned to trek out to the plane to salvage what I could and propped a note on the pillow beside Jessie in case she woke. Leaving her felt like ripping a chunk of hair off my face, but I forced myself to go. She had supplies in that plane that I wanted. And I needed fresh air to set my head on straight.

Waking up beside her with a raging hard on for the fourth day in a row had almost proved too much temptation. Dick in hand, I'd squeezed to the point of pain, groaning against the need to take. Dominate. Barely hanging on by a thread, I'd rolled from the warmth of my bed needing a cold shower.

Cold fucking air would have to do.

Stepping into the outdoors took me into a bone-stabbing cold I hadn't felt since attempting to scale Everest. Definitely below normal for Alaska in October. Ghostly silence hovered even as stray snowflakes fell, coating my eyelashes and beard. I pulled old Ray's sled off the back of the lean-to and pressed on through the snow and trees, my breath fogging, the frigid stillness enough to wake a man from his lust.

Fucking cold.

Fucking perfect.

My blood pumped, but I kept at a slower than usual pace, needing to take it easy with my knee and not wanting to overheat and end up sweating out in the below freezing temperatures.

The plane lay half-buried in snow, but I didn't have any trouble getting the back door open. Pulling things up and out of the plane on its side didn't prove as easy, but I managed to get a few cases and boxes loaded onto the sled.

Jessie hadn't moved when I returned, so I unloaded and headed back, taking three trips before needing a break.

I sat and stared at her like a perv while shoveling down stew I'd made the day before, eating the last of my stale sourdough biscuits I'd made the day before she'd crashed. My nose eventually thawed, as did my fingers and toes. Figuring I'd done enough for the day, I tried my phone again.

Nothing.

Unable to focus on anything but Jessie, I laid down beside her and entwined my fingers through hers. "How long are you going to sleep, hmm? You're driving me mad with worry, mad with lust, mad with the fact I'm responsible for you right now and my hands are fucking tied."

Of course, she didn't reply, but I'd started to spill. Why the fuck not finish? Maybe it would quiet the fear eating away at my guts.

"I came out here so I wouldn't have to be responsible for anyone ever again," I told her quietly, my gaze studying how her pale eyelashes fanned above her high cheek bones. "I killed three people."

My confession hung heavy in the air, but there was no judgement, no recoiling, or disgusted looks.

"Engine malfunction, but it was my reckless error that sent us into the mountainside." I swallowed as guilt clawed at my gut as it always did whenever I saw the memories flashing through my mind. "I was the only survivor. I should have been the only one to die."

Silence eventually drove me onward.

"My brother's fiancé lost her life because of me, and now I am nothing to him—as I should be. He won't speak to me, won't look at me, won't go to our parents when he knows I'm there. But I would do the same. The lawsuits from the other two families went in my favor thanks to my friend Rian, but I still sold off a shit ton of stocks and bonds to give them some sort of repayment on my own. Cash, but hardly an easement of grief. Can't buy a soul back. Cash isn't that powerful."

I smoothed back her hair as I'd done dozens of times in the previous couple of days, letting out a sigh.

"Did you know I was the one who wired money to you? Has it helped? I hoped you'd be able to buy back your dad's plane. Were you able to get a lawyer and take care of whatever asshole it is who's trying to ruin your family's company?"

Her eyelid twitched, and I propped up on an elbow, studying her face.

"Jessie?" I whispered and held my breath, my heart thudding the seconds as they ticked by.

She made no move toward waking, and settling back down onto my side, I shoved a hand beneath my bearded cheek and continued to watch her. Maybe my voice would draw her back…

I continued to spill the shit from the previous two years. My face plastered on the east coast papers and media news outlets. Named an adrenaline junkie, which was true, but the dug-up stories from my younger twenties morphed beyond truth until they had painted me as a careless punk who lived on the edge, tempting fate and death regardless of those who'd entrusted their lives to my care.

While my mother had insisted I fight back, I hadn't been

able to rouse the energy. I wasn't worthy of forgiveness, wasn't worthy, period.

Leaving had been the best thing I'd done.

"And I found you," I told Jessie, pulling the bear skin up a bit higher atop my quilt. "You're making me question all sorts of shit in my head, vixen. Not sure what to think or how to feel. How about you wake up and help me figure it out?"

She didn't listen, the stubborn woman, and I eventually closed my eyes, giving into my emotional and physical exhaustion.

21

JESSIE

Warmth cocooned me, and I breathed in the memory of Brock's scent, his groan tingling arousal through my aching body.

Aching.

I grimaced as pain radiated from my head to my toes, but the muscle contraction between my eyebrows hurt bad enough I didn't do more than breathe. Woozy to the point of nausea, I inhaled and exhaled steady, trying to clear the exhausted fuzziness from my brain.

A groan sounded, the guttural tone slickening my pussy.

Warm—too warm.

I blinked, bringing into focus a cabin's roof I recognized from a fire's flickering flames.

Brock.

"Fuck," he whispered harshly, the mattress shifting beside me.

I'm in his bed...

The plane crash came back with a flash, and I relived the few seconds after the explosion, the trees, the rush of the ground coming at me—

"Jessie." My name on Brock's lips, the sounds of wet fucking… *Schlick, schlick…*

I managed to turn my head, biting back a whimper at the pain behind my eyes. His broad back rested beside me, his left arm working, moving the blankets atop us.

My pussy pulsed as I realized he jerked off beside me—to thoughts of me.

Half dead, I should have been pissed, sickened, but I drank in his moans, his curses, wishing pain didn't riddle me to the point of not wanting to move.

He fucked his hand—not my listless body when he very well could have taken advantage of my state. That idea of being used without consent shouldn't have turned me on even more, but the idea of the feral side of Brock I'd experienced last time when I'd landed…

"Fuuuuck…" Brock drug out the word, his hips jerking. A grunt, a curse, and he shuddered. "Shit."

Too warm.

Tired.

My eyelids dragged shut even though my body roused with need to feel him rutting between my thighs. Darkness closed in over the image in my mind of his face painted in blood.

Consciousness returned.

Hot breath and soft beard on my neck. Heavy arm draped over my belly. Hairy thigh propped against mine. Hard cock digging into my hip.

Brock.

I'd woken the same once before weeks earlier, and instant

panic had sent me slipping from his bed and sneaking off to take to the skies as he'd slept.

No chance in hell of me doing the same. Pain still wracked my head like a migraine from hell, rendering the rest of my body useless. And I knew my Beaver lay in shambles.

I wouldn't be going anywhere.

I don't want to.

The thought rang clearly in my head, and I closed my eyes again, soaking in the warmth of Brock's body pressed against mine, the scent of firewood and smoked meat. Musk and man. Comfort and safety.

How long had I been out? Two hours? Ten days? I had no fucking clue. I'd known nothing but darkness, zero consciousness except for the few seconds of reality when he'd jacked off beside me.

Arousal sprung to life again, but wooziness slammed into me as I attempted to tilt my head his way. I held still, replaying those few minutes in my mind.

A sigh shuddered through me, and his heavy breath stopped short. Time stilled, the fire crackling a short distance away.

Slowly, Brock backed away from my body, and I forced my head to turn as he left me cold.

Thick lashes framed eyes squinted from sleep. "You're awake," he breathed the words.

"Yeah," I rasped, the dryness of my throat coming to light in my head.

"Are you alright? Can you see okay? How's your head?"

I blinked, trying to focus on his face as he went fuzzy as shit. "Head hurts," I whispered, closing my eyes.

The mattress shifted, and I peeled an eyelid open to find him rolling off the bed.

Naked as a jay.

Ass flexing as he took two steps, cheeks spreading as he bent to retrieve something off the floor. Standing, his torso rippled—and he half-turned, offering me a view of his hard cock.

Moisture rose to coat my mouth, and I stared until he pulled pants up to his waist.

"Jessie."

I lifted my focus up over the rest of him as he turned, reaching toward the small shelf above the bed. The scent of him swarmed over me, and my thighs pressed together on their own—no pain down there at all.

"Here." He put a spoon to my lips, and I sucked the water down.

"More." The bit barely coated my tongue, and thirst like I'd never known rose with a choking need.

He offered another spoonful. "Want to try to sit up a bit so you can drink from the cup?"

"Yeah." With his help, we managed to get me into a reclining position, propped up on his only pillow and an extra blanket. My head pounded to the point I couldn't keep my eyes open, but the rest of my body felt okay as I drank down the entire glass of water, its coolness sliding clear to my empty stomach.

I'm naked...

Eyelid cracking open again, I glanced down at the sheet he'd pulled up to rest over my bare breasts. "How long?"

"Five days."

"Fuck." Weakness plagued me alongside the debilitating pain in my head.

"How bad is the pain?"

"Bad," I managed through grit teeth.

"I have morphine."

I listened as he shuffled around the cabin but couldn't focus on anything.

"Ready?"

"Mmm," I agreed.

The blankets shifted, the cool air sliding over my side.

He slid a needle into my thigh close to my ass, but I barely felt it past the pounding between my temples.

"Hit your head pretty damn hard," he said, covering me back up. "Laceration bled like hell. Had me worried, but not as bad as your refusing to wake."

He rustled around a bit and the mattress once more shifted as the morphine did its work. Slow hazy numbness drifted over me until my brow smoothed beneath his brushing my hair back from my forehead, and I sighed, my body going slack.

"Tell me what happened," I whispered.

22

BROCK

She lay propped up and still, breathing quietly while I perched on the edge of the bed and told her about the crash, and I couldn't tell if she slipped back into unconsciousness or not. I kept talking, though, sharing every detail I could remember while gently working my fingers through her hair, smoothing my fingertips against her scalp.

Finally, a sigh shuddered through her, and I fell silent, only having gotten to day two of her out cold in my bed, letting her know all about my own head being a fucked up mess of worry waiting for her to wake.

I left out the parts about my washing her body and getting hard as hell.

"Why'd you come out here knowing the storm headed in?" I whispered, gliding my thumb across her chin, slightly parting her lips, and giving myself a boner over thoughts of sliding my dick between them.

"Midnight Sun Charter keeps its promises." Her words slurred a bit—but at least she'd answered.

"It could have waited."

"I didn't want to. Needed to get away."

Studying her lax face, I considered her words. Had the money I'd sent not helped? "Did you go to court?"

"Yeah." Jessie shifted, a frown denting her brow and smoothing once she stilled again. "I won."

A grin damn near split my face. "Congrats."

"Thanks." She tried to open her eyes and focus on me, and blinked a few times before giving up and closing them once more. "He's pissed, though. Can you believe that asshole tried to pay me off?" A soft laugh passed her lips. "He thought a pile of money would get him in my pants. Talk about the backfire of the century. My lawyer buried Cort, and Midnight Sun is mine. I used his own bribe money to beat him. Pay off my debt." She swallowed, a frown flitting over her brow. "Bought myself a new truck. Paid off my Beaver." Her voice broke.

Cort.

The asshole wanting to get into her pants… Cort Endsley.

"Shit," I muttered.

Jessie blinked up at me as the pieces of what I knew, what she'd told me slid into place inside my head.

"Cort Endsley is the asshole you've been talking about."

She nodded even though I hadn't asked a question.

I leaned down to kiss the frown from her forehead, my thoughts running. "I got ahold of him after your crash. He's sending a plane out here to get you once the storm lets up."

"*If* he follows through, I'm not leaving with him," Jessie said, and I sat back to find her gaze plastered to my face even though her pupils blew out from the morphine. "He said I'd be sorry outside the courthouse—I don't trust him or any offer of help."

"You don't think…" I recalled the loud bang seconds before Jessie's plane had gone down.

"What?"

Not knowing how bad the backstory of him and her parents were, I considered my thoughts, but didn't want to make her worry. Fuck knew she had to have enough on her mind being stuck out in the wilderness with me.

"What?" she pressed when I didn't continue.

"Might be ugly…"

"What?"

"You told me you thought he was responsible for your parents' accident," I said, keeping my voice level.

She nodded.

"Does he hate your family name enough to try the same with you?"

Her brow furrowed at my murmured suggestion. "I don't know what the fuck his problem is, but I wouldn't put it past him. He's got to feel like a fool for losing to me in court because of that money he gave me."

"Any idea what the explosion was before you went down?" I asked rather than focus on the fact she thought he'd given her the cash I'd had deposited into her account.

"Something in the engine, but other than that, no clue. Happened so damn fast…"

"Fuck." I sat back, running my hands through my hair. "Guess he probably won't be keeping his promise to get you the hell out of here then, huh?"

"Probably not." A snorted laugh escaped her nose. "Looks like you're stuck with me."

I was fine as fuck with that idea. Seeing Jessie in my bed filled me with a primal need to keep her there. Mark her with my teeth, my scent. Let the other predators of the world know she belonged to me.

Belonged…

That echoed word slammed into my head with enough force to rattle me clear to my bones.

"What?" she whispered, her brow furrowing.

I couldn't tell her the truth. Jessie Blacke stood on her own two feet, the stubborn vixen, and I was a rich boy, far from her idea of a good man. "Nothing," I muttered, shoving thoughts of claiming her from my head. "Want me to power up my sat phone? You ought to call family and friends to let them know you're okay since Cort won't be reaching out to anyone, I'm sure."

Pain flickered in her eyes, and not from her head. "Don't have any family—but I should call Foster, at least. He'll be worried sick.

My cell only had a fraction of its power left, but service showed, and I managed to put through the call for her. I moved off to the kitchen area to give her some sense of privacy. She left Foster a detailed message, telling him she was fine. Telling him to not worry, and that she would get in touch with him in a few days.

She wants to stay.

A strange flutter woke in my chest.

"Want some stew?" I asked after she hung up, my back still toward her, trying not to grin like a fucking moron.

"Sure."

I started out offering spoonfuls of stew to Jessie, but she frowned and insisted on feeding herself even though her hands shook and she ended up with stew juices running down her chin back into the bowl she clutched to her breast.

She allowed me to watch only for all of three minutes before grumbling about my having something better to do.

Stubborn vixen, indeed.

I left her side, grabbed my cell, and went out into the

cold, the gray skies clear enough I didn't expect the snow to return in the immediate future.

Rian picked up after the first ring. "The fuck, man! You okay?"

I chuckled. "Yeah. Doing good, actually."

He tossed out a few more rapid-fire questions which I answered, typical of his FBI ass. No, I didn't miss social media, but that question gave me the opening to get into why I called. I briefly explained about Jessie to save the battery, but only that she was my pilot, my only connection to the outside world, that she'd crashed.

Rian's tone changed from teasing to serious, and he promised to help a brother out. "You fuck her?"

Of course, he had to go there. "Yeah."

He snorted. "How'd it feel to bury your dick in pussy after months on end?"

"I went without for two goddamn years," I reminded him, hugging myself against the biting wind whipping at my hair.

"So, you're calling me to help get her out of the sticks— she that bad you want her gone?"

"That *good* I sent her five-hundred grand to get her out of debt, fight the asshole in court, and help keep her promise to her dad to keep the family business going after he passed."

"Oh."

"Yeah," I murmured, rethinking that *belonged* thing.

"You found her, huh? The one?"

"Don't know."

He snorted again. "You're all done."

"Do me a favor?" I asked rather than discuss how I felt about Jessie. I had called for a reason, after all. "Check into Endsley. I want everything you've got on him—especially anything related to the Blacke family."

"You got it. And do you need a lift for your woman?"

I ought to have replied yes, for him to get her out as quickly as possible considering she'd gone down in a plane crash five days earlier and ought to get checked out by a doctor, but I hesitated. She seemed to be doing well. Eating, no evidence of head trauma beyond the bump and healing laceration. Swelling down, pupils perfectly normal when not high on morphine… She'd also told Foster she'd give him a call when she was ready to get flown out.

"I'll let you know."

"You got it."

23

JESSIE

Brock had given me the money. Not Cort.

I'd devoured the stew while he spoke on the phone right outside the front door, my slurping keeping me from hearing his conversation. But then I finished, resting the bowl on my lap.

And I heard every word from that point on.

Why hadn't he told me? Why keep it a secret?

I started to ponder those questions, but Brock came back into the cabin, letting in a blast of cold air.

"You okay?" He kept his focus on my face while locking us in and striding my way.

I nodded, fighting to focus on his eyes as they flitted to my empty bowl.

"Too much? Want more?"

"I'm good." My gaze tracked him as he took my bowl to the bucket he used to wash up the dishes. What was his angle? He didn't need to buy his way into my pants—I couldn't keep the damn things on around him. Even doped up on morphine, my body longed to have him closer. Wrapped up in the warm blankets with me.

While the thought of having him between my thighs tingled need through me, I didn't have the energy to fuck.

Maybe he was just a good guy. Saw a need and wasn't stingy with money he had to blow on cases of Coke and boxes of Snickers. Or, maybe he liked me, and kept the truth bomb for the perfect moment for a bribe or something.

I hated that I questioned his integrity, didn't trust his intentions, but I hadn't found a man worth trusting since my dad—and even he had let me down with things I hadn't known about until long after he and Mom had passed.

"Why'd you give me that money?" I heard myself ask.

Brock paused in washing my bowl, but finished and returned to sit beside me, bringing the scent of the ozone and outdoors with him. "You heard?"

I nodded, blinking to better focus on his dark eyes as his gaze slid down over my face and lingered on my lips.

"Because you needed help," he murmured. "Because you're good at what you do and don't deserve to have all you've worked for toppled to the ground because of one greedy asshole."

My throat tightened.

"And I like you, Jessie—really like you." Brock's gaze returned to my eyes, the intense study tingling my body again. "I knew if I offered, though, you wouldn't have accepted my help. You're strong and are independent to a fault, so I didn't bother giving you the option to reject a rich boy wanting to help in the only way he could."

I believed him. Every rumbled word. "Thank you," I whispered.

Silence settled except for the crackling of the fire as we stared at one another. Emotions and thoughts swarmed through a haze of morphine. I liked him, too. Maybe too much. Enough I didn't care about the outside world, only being shut up in quiet and safety with him.

Brock eventually tore his focus off my face to glance down over me. "How are you feeling? Need anything?"

You. I shook my head, and he left me to stoke the fire.

My gaze tracked after him as I shifted down from my reclining position to rest. He moved with assurance, as though on autopilot, no move wasted. A few logs on the fire. My bowl and spoon dried and put away. Dish towel and rag hung by the fire to dry.

"Why are you here, Brock?" I asked, needing to know what drove him. Maybe figure out what drew me to him.

He paused from turning down the lamp on the small table, his back to me and shoulders hunching. "I was a private pilot back in Boston. Went on one too many joy rides. Crashed two years ago on a flight to Nova Scotia, and even though the evidence didn't prove pilot error, I still feel responsible."

Shit. The reason for his fear while flying into the bush made perfect sense. I expected that had been his first flight since the accident, and I couldn't imagine the guilt...

Brock stretched out beside me on his back, his focus on the ceiling.

"Killed my brother's fiancé, and I might as well have killed myself since I'm dead to him, now. I gladly paid the money I'd been sued for to the other families, wishing I could have done more. But money can't buy everything. Not life. Not the removal of guilt. Not peace."

I slid my hand over his arm to where his fingers laced above his navel. He disentangled his fingers and wound his through mine. "You're finding it here, aren't you?" I asked, my voice hushed.

He turned his head my way, dark eyes once more studying my face. "I'm finding a new me here—one ruled by the wilderness and instinct. I wouldn't call it peace, but it's a peaceful existence if that makes sense."

"It helps being at the top of the food chain," I said with a smirk, remembering the blood and carcass of the predator that had brought on the instincts that made him devour me.

"I'm afraid of grizzlies. They scare the shit out of me."

"I'm afraid of being helpless and dependent on others."

"You hate how you're feeling right now, don't you?"

I nodded even though a part of me liked having a man who wanted to look out for me. "Sorry for cramping your space. Will your friend get me out of here soon if Foster can't?"

"As soon as possible, yes, but he's taking a day first to check into Cort. I hope you don't mind I told him some of the background you told me—he's an FBI agent back in Boston."

"It's okay." I closed my eyes as exhaustion sank my body deeper into the soft mattress.

Brock brushed my hair back, leaned over, and kissed my forehead. "Rest up, vixen. I want to see you up on your own two feet, bristling, and ready to go kick some ass."

He wants me gone.

That thought lingered long after I regretted not telling Foster to come pick me up the minute the unsettled weather allowed.

24

BROCK

I woke with Jessie's back pressed against my chest, one arm beneath my head in place of the pillow she used, my other arm banded around her waist holding her tight in a possessive hold.

Belonged…

The word echoed, and I closed my eyes against the still dark interior of the cabin, taking stock of the colder air nipping my nose. I needed to stoke the fire, but the warmth of her against my front, the softness of her belly against my hand, the natural, sweet scent of her flooding my nose…

My too-early morning wood loved the silkiness of her leg, swelling as I inhaled her, filling my lungs. Within seconds, my balls ached, and I fought the need to grind against her, seeking release.

I should have rolled the other way and emptied my balls into my hand like I'd done the morning before but couldn't tear myself away. Face nuzzling against her hair, I soaked her in, trying to imprint the feel of her beneath my hand into my brain for the lonely winter ahead.

Warmth cocooned us, but I couldn't let the cabin grow too cold before she woke.

Choosing to not be a selfish prick, I shifted to move away, but she clasped her hand over mine.

"Don't go," she whispered, and I snuggled back in, rubbing my aching shaft against her lower ass.

"You're killing me, Jessie," I muttered against her shoulder, nipping at the tender flesh.

She reached around her hip and I inched back to give her the access she wanted—her hand grasped around my dick, and I groaned, rubbing my lips along her shoulder.

"Fuck, vixen."

Slow, gentle jacking brought me to the point of exploding in a matter of seconds.

"Gonna come if you keep this up," I rumbled a warning against her ear.

She shifted and pressed her ass against me, notching the head of my dick in the wet heat of her pussy.

I cursed a mean streak through clenched teeth as she backed against me, stuffing herself full with my throbbing dick. "You feel so fucking good."

"Mmm." She arched her back, her fingers entwining with mine over her belly. "Just … be careful. Head hurts."

"Always," I whispered against her ear, and began rocking in and out of her tight sheath, my pre-cum and her arousal making for one hell of a sticky, slick mess. So good. So damn good *together*. "The things you do to me, Jessie. Goddamn."

My balls tingled, but I held off, sliding our clasped hands down far enough my palm pressed against her clit. She shuddered and sighed, and I kept my ass in a steady but gentle flexing, the drag and suck of her tight pussy on my dick rolling my eyes back into my head.

Heat rushed through me, my heart pounded—better than any fucking workout known to man.

Wet pussy. Sweet, sweet woman. Whimpers and pebbled skin.

I loosened my hold on her hand to cup her core while fucking between my fingers, my lips, tongue, and teeth eating at every inch of her neck and shoulder. The need to plunder, plow into her, shoot my cum against her womb rose inside me like Griz to his hind legs.

"Fuck, Jessie—need to fuck you. Need to feel you come around my dick, baby." I rubbed her clit with slickened fingertips, her inner walls clenching at me.

"Harder," she gasped out, her back arching.

"No," I tossed back through clenched teeth.

"Give it to me, Brock. Please. I need—"

I thrust, stealing her breath even though I could have gone deep enough to slide her across my bed.

"More."

"Goddamnit." Thrumming her clit, I gave her more—but still held back, trying like hell to not jostle her around too much, only thrusting hard the final inch or two against her womb.

"Oh… Fuck, Brock." She groaned, her back arching to fuck herself harder with every thrust of my hips. "So good… Brock!" Her shriek hit me like a gale force, her pussy squeezing the life out of my dick—I fucking lost it.

I pounded into her, grunting like a goddamn, mindless animal, my palm once more clasped over her clit, her pussy.

Mine. Fucking mine.

Hot. Wet. So damn tight. Couldn't get deep enough, couldn't work my way into her sou—

I came with a roar, bucking into her soaked body, sporadic spurts of cum shooting deep inside her. Blood rushed through my arteries, thrumming in time with the heartbeat in my ears. One last twitch through my dick, and I lay lax behind her, still holding her tight, my ears ringing.

Jessie shivered, and I yanked the covers up that had gotten jostled near our knees.

"Fuck. Sorry," I muttered, holding her close to warm her.

"Don't be."

Wetness leaked around my dick still shoved inside her, and I pressed closer, trying to keep it there.

She giggled.

"What's so funny?" I muttered against the back of her head.

"You've become a feral beast out here in the back woods."

"Only when it comes to you." I nipped her shoulder with a growl, and pulled out, rolling from beneath the blankets. "Don't move."

"Can't," she replied with a sigh.

Enough light shone through the window I could make out her white-blonde hair on my pillow. The white sheets. My beautiful angel.

Heart light, I hurried to grab a few tissues from one of the boxes she'd flown in with her.

"I got it," she said, reaching for them when I went to clean between her thighs.

Guess my days of caring for her are at an end.

The thought stung like a bitch when months earlier, I'd have been relieved.

Turning to give her privacy, I fought the furrow in my brow, wiped off my dick, and tossed the tissue into the bit of glowing embers in the fireplace. Squatting, I grabbed some kindling and the poker, getting some flames high enough to lick at bigger logs and warm the cabin up.

The crackle and pop of the piece of pine I set atop the embers eased the frown between my eyebrows, and I stared at the flickering orange and yellow as it rose, warming my face and hands.

Jessie tossed her tissues at the fire, but they fell short. Our cum smeared my fingers as I picked them up and fed them to the flames. Musk and sweetness…

I sniffed my fingers, breathing us deep into my lungs, my mouth watering and dick twitching.

"You're a damn animal," she huffed with a laugh as I sucked my fingers clean of our cum.

Standing and turning, I saw her stretched on her back, a shade of rose coloring her cheeks, her eyes more alert than I'd seen since the accident. The sheet slipped beneath one of her breasts, the nipple beaded.

I found myself prowling toward her, and she shivered beneath my stare. "It's cold," I grumbled, tugging the bear skin off her body rather than cover her up.

She didn't reply, and I grasped the quilt, pulling it, too, toward the foot of the bed. Nothing but a sheet hid her from me.

A damn animal—I wanted it all.

One yank of the sheet left her naked and shivering. "Spread your legs," I rasped out, my stare on the soft blonde hair between her thighs.

She did as told, the reddened, swollen petals of her pussy opening to let me see heaven.

I climbed between her thighs, hungry to taste her, hoping she hadn't gotten every drop with the tissues.

Sprawled on my stomach, I buried my nose in her pussy and breathed her—us—in, a growl rumbling my chest. Running my nose up to her clit, I flicked out my tongue, my dick swelling again at the lingering trace of our cum clinging to her inner walls.

Jessie sighed, her thighs going lax in my hold even as she grasped at my hair.

"You like my tongue in you."

"God, yes," she moaned as I shoved my tongue back in, licking as deeply into her as I could go. "I like your dick, too."

Fuck.

A nip at each swollen labia, a kiss to her clit, and I crawled up her body, my dick once again hard and aching. "Taking you again."

A soft smile curved her lips as she reached for me.

"Is your head okay?" I asked, notching a mere inch inside her tight body.

"I'll be fine."

I flexed my ass—and a snuffle against the front door froze my muscles from burying inside her.

"Brock?" Jessie cupped my scruffy cheek as I strained to listen, ears ringing, breath held.

Another snuffle … a brush of something heavy against the wall.

I jerked my head toward the door, staring at the planks as though I could see through the fucking thing. My heart rate hitched up, shriveling my dick to nothing. Still, I didn't move, ignoring my limp dick as it slipped from Jessie's body.

"What is it?" she whispered, her fingers grasping at my shoulders.

"Bear," I rasped, swallowing against the clench of my gut.

Fucking fear.

Another snuffle. A snort.

Nothing sounded from outside for a full minute as I planked over Jessie, my muscles tense and shaking, my jaw clenched, my gaze tracking along the cabin's interior, waiting for another rustle or snort.

One of the fire's logs popped, jackknifing my pulse, and I sat back on my haunches, shoulders hitched up near my straining ears.

Jessie shivered in my periphery, and I hopped off the bed, yanking the covers up over her nakedness.

Belonged…

Nothing would touch her. She was mine to protect. Mine…

Darkness I'd become familiar with rose inside me, a welcome shroud to the fear. I stalked toward the front door, pulled my rifle from its hooks overhead, and stood waiting for the fucker outside to tempt fate. The cold didn't touch me as heat steadily pumped through my veins in a rage of need to take. Spill blood. Taste his flesh on my tongue.

A full five minutes passed, the sounds of our breathing and the fire loud in my ears, and the adrenaline rush faded, relaxing my shoulders even as my mouth watered to taste the coppery tang of his life's blood.

"He's gone."

I ignored Jessie's murmur and stayed put for a few more minutes, my gut hard as a rock, mouth still salivating.

"Brock."

Images of Griz rising on his hind legs, drool dripping from his jowls filled my mind, and I tightened my grip on my rifle, brow still dented in a deep groove. I would cut him from throat to belly. Rip his guts out and tear into his flesh with my teeth. I would—

"Brock. Please. I need you."

Jessie's words filtered through the need for blood running through my head, and I blinked the front door into focus.

"Hey."

I glanced over my shoulder to find her buried in blankets, her face pale, eyes wide.

I need you.

"Shit. You okay?" I hurried toward her, leaning my rifle against the wall beside the headboard, all thoughts of hunting sliding beneath my concern for her.

"I'll be better once you're back in bed with me."

"Fucking bear," I muttered, glancing once more at the door.

"He can't get in. We're safe." She clutched at my arm. "Get in here and warm me up."

The sudden need for silken skin wrapped around me tore my focus off the need for war between predators, and I burrowed beneath the blankets.

"Shit!" She shrieked as I pulled her against my body. "You're fucking cold!"

I buried my nose in her neck, her laughter keeping me rooted in the present, dispelling the fear I thought I'd mastered.

So much for my peaceful existence.

25

JESSIE

He'd claimed to want to see me on my own two feet, but telling Brock I needed him had been what pulled him from wherever he'd gone in his head. I imagined the fear he'd felt while facing the grizzly he'd been lucky enough to kill but couldn't find fault with him. What man wouldn't be on the verge of shitting his pants having gunned down a bear that size from mere feet away?

What man wouldn't relive that moment when faced with another beast prowling around his cabin?

Brock had been lucky to survive.

I'd been lucky to survive the wreckage he'd told me about.

As though fate had plans for us…

I considered that thought as his body eventually warmed beside me, but exhaustion tugged me back beneath its heavy blanket before I could decide if I wanted the same or not.

I woke first the next morning, watching Brock sleep, his dark head propped up on his bent arm since he insisted I take the pillow. Dark hair curled above his ears, the wild waves atop untamable and sexy as hell. My fingers itched to feel the strands, and I found myself running my hand over his head.

"Mmm," he rumbled, shifting to draw me closer with an arm like a band of steel.

"Sorry. Didn't mean to wake you."

"Don't mind." Eyes still closed, he palmed my ass and tucked a hairy thigh between my legs, snuggling his semi against my core. "Did I die in my sleep? Cuz I've dreamed about waking up like this all summer long."

I huffed a quiet laugh, ruffling his hair as he nosed my neck. Warmth flooded my entire body, and while I should have been focused on getting back to my life back home, finding a way to rebuild my company, I found myself content.

"Thank you."

He stilled his lips perusal of my neck and pulled back, blinking sleeping, dark eyes at me. "For?"

"Keeping me alive." My throat tightened in sudden emotion I couldn't explain, and I pulled him close, pressing my lips against his, uncaring of morning breath. "The money. Making me laugh. Listening. Accepting my stubborn ass as-is."

"Fucking love that about you."

"All the toe-curling orgasms," I continued, my lips twitching.

"Mmm." He nipped my jaw and rolled me beneath him, his shifting hips rubbing his hardening length over my wet folds. "I could give you one or three right now if you want."

Another laugh began, but he kissed it away and slid inside my body as though he belonged there.

By the time he left me lax and sated to build up the fire

and make coffee, I wondered if he didn't. For the first time, I didn't push against emotion. Didn't tell myself to keep in my head rather than let my heart get caught up in a tailwind.

I crawled from his bed to relieve myself in his piss pot as he called it, and even though he'd helped me out of bed to do so the day before, I hadn't made the connection that he'd been caring for me while I'd been out cold. In a coma for a few days—my body must have relieved itself without conscious thought.

Heat flooded my cheeks, but I pushed away the embarrassment, choosing to focus instead on the fact that he cared enough to pull me from the wreckage and keep me safe and as clean as possible until I woke.

Maybe he'd gotten caught up in emotion, too.

I crawled back into the warmth of the bed and watched him whip up a batch of pancakes in peaceful quiet, the wood stove he'd fired up to cook quickly heating the cabin's small interior. He seemed to have found what he'd been looking for, and I had to give the man credit. He'd lasted longer than I expected. Seemed more at ease than what I figured I'd find after weeks in solitude. The heaviness that had fallen over him when the bear had come sniffing around should have worried me—his singular mindset on protecting his territory, taking down whatever predator outdoors thought to question his dominance.

A shiver licked at my skin at the truth of his instinct turning me on—even though he'd given me those three promised orgasms. Once again, I remembered the blood coating his face and chest, the animal instinct in his eyes as he'd strode from the water and fucked me right there on the beach, his arms a band around me, his body like an unshakable mountain. Strong. Unwavering.

Brock Charran was one hell of a man with layers that

intrigued me. I wanted to know it all, and over the next two days, I probed, and he shared. We spoke of our pasts, our heartaches, and wins.

The bear stayed away, giving us quiet and rest while waiting for the weather to clear again.

The Alaskan weather sat in a pattern of unrest, high winds and snow squalls buffeting the cabin for two days. Brock got ahold of his friend back east during a break in the sky's unrest, but unless he sent out the coast guard, no one could get to us for at least a week.

Seeing as how Midnight Sun Charter lay in pieces down by the river, I didn't need to rush to get back. I called old man Foster again, and I spoke briefly with him, refusing his insistence he find a way to get out to pick me up. Last I'd seen or heard, he couldn't see worth a shit—it's why his own bush plane and chopper sat untouched, unused since the summer before.

No Cort.

No worries.

Voracious dick and rest.

Why would I want to leave?

I sat on his lone chair at the table while he perched on a log he'd cut to height, eating a one-pot, skillet chicken and potatoes meal he'd made on the wood stove which had warmed the cabin toasty enough I sat in one of his oversized shirts and sweatpants tied around my waist. At least my socks survived, but I kept a pair of his woolen ones atop mine beneath the table.

He'd finished digging through the rubble I didn't yet wish to see, finding the broken cooler I'd brought the frozen chicken in. Seeing as how frigid temperatures kept us indoors, the cutlets had stayed frozen solid. Bear tracks surrounded the wreckage, he'd told me, but the beast hadn't managed to get in through the door Brock had managed to shut a few days earlier.

His moan at the first bite glued my gaze to his face and warmed me through. My appetite had returned in full force, my headaches down to a dull throb in the evenings. I ate while watching him enjoy his first chicken in months.

"How is it?" I asked, smirking.

"Unbelievable. Forgot how damn good chicken is."

"You could get a few cluckers out here. Build them a fortified coop."

"Bears would get after them," he said quietly before shoveling another mouthful between his lips.

His fear hadn't come sniffing around the cabin in bodily form again, and although I personally knew others who kept chickens off grid, I let the matter go.

Chirps sounded outside the door, and Brock left his plate half-full, grabbed a cracker from the tin, and stepped outside into the bitterness to feed his little chickadee while his own meal grew cold.

Thirty seconds or so later, he sat once more, and I shivered in the blast of cold air the door opening and closing had let in.

"Sorry," he muttered, digging back into his food.

Smirking and falling hard for his softness for a little bird, I focused on my food rather than bring up his soft, squishy insides and embarrass the hell out of him. Caring for Chick more than the chicken he'd been salivating over while cooking.

"You're the first person who's learned the truth about what I did without judging me."

His statement drew my head up, and I considered his tone, his words. "It was an accident, pure and simple, Brock. I'm not going to judge what I wasn't there to witness. I didn't manage to land my own plane from whatever malfunction—or tampering—had sent me careening into the ground. Shit happens, some intentional, some not, and we react with instinct born or learned from years of practice. You've flown longer than I have, probably twice the hours I've logged. I'm sure you did all you could."

"Can't help but question that every day, though."

I could imagine. "Do you believe in fate?" I asked, setting aside my fork and leaning onto the table.

"I used to—until that shit happened. Doesn't seem right that fate would make me her bitch in that way. Killing my future sister-in-law. Two old friends from school." He shook his head, pushing his empty plate away, his troubled gaze finding my face.

"Fate willed it—so let the guilt rest on that bitch. You care for little Chick like he's your closest friend."

"He is." Brock's crooked smile turned my insides to butter and fluttered my heart inside my chest.

"Those protective instincts for a mere fluff of feather and bone are nothing compared to what you feel for humanity. You did all you could, Brock. Focus on that rather than the loss."

He grasped my hand and pulled me off the chair onto his lap, his focus on my mouth. "How do straight-forward words out of your mouth make more sense to me than any of the therapists I've sat with for hours on end?"

I shrugged and ran my fingers through his hair, smiling as he closed his eyes and leaned into my touch like a needy cat. "Just state things as I see them."

"Mmm." He enjoyed the hell out of my fingernails scratching his scalp for a few seconds before pinning me in place with his dark eyes. "And how do you see us?"

Us.

Fucking loaded question. Was there an us? Certainly felt like it, all cozy in his cabin in the woods, snowed in, with nothing to do but eat, sleep, and fuck. But I had a business back home. An insurance claim to file. Another plane to purchase and start over rebuilding Midnight Sun Charter.

"Not sure how to answer that one," I finally said, hating the disappointment in his eyes. "Things are … complicated right now, you know?"

"Yeah." He let out a huff while shifting me around to straddle his lap. "Just enjoying the hell out of you, Jessie. Not so keen on some other guy flying out here to take you away from me."

My lips twitched at his rumbly growl and obvious alpha nature coming out. "You're a contradiction—but I like you, Brock."

"Pretty sure I already told you I like you, too," he said, a twinkle lighting his eyes as his focus slipped once more to my mouth.

"So how about you kiss me, and we can forget everything else for a sh—"

He stole my words with a heated kiss, and damn near stole my heart with the emotion he poured into me with every brush of fingers, whisper of praise, and every nip of his teeth.

Leaving Brock to the wild, to the winter months of solitude ahead, sent an ache through my chest I didn't understand but sure as hell wanted to.

26

BROCK

The bear showed up a half hour after I fried up some bacon over the open fire, his scratching at the wall alongside my chimney and snorts pissing me off more than bringing the fear from a few days earlier. Even though I had more than my own life to look after, Jessie's presence kept me rooted in the present, helped keep me calm.

I popped a window open and shot into the sky since he stood out of sight at the back of the cabin, but he rounded the house, lumbering away. While I didn't need more meat, I'd had about enough of his sniffing around. I chambered another round and took a shot the second he offered a glimpse of his front shoulder.

"Did you get him?" Jessie asked from behind me.

The fucker had stumbled, so I know I'd landed a hit. "Pretty sure, yeah. I'm going out to finish this," I told her while locking the window back up. "Tracking will be easy in this snow."

"I'll keep the fire warm for you." Her smile brought light to my insides.

"Keep my bed warm," I said, grabbing my boots from alongside hers by the front door.

Jessie laughed, the welcomed sound making me grin. "I'll just lay there and touch myself while thinking about you."

I growled. "Goddamnit, woman." Sitting, I eyed her in my clothes while pulling my boots on. "You do that, and I want to hear you screaming my name clear up through the hills."

She threw herself into my arms when I stood, plastering her mouth to mine. "Be careful," she whispered, clasping my fuzzy cheeks in her hands while I palmed her thighs. "I'm starting to like having you all up my ass."

My dick twitched. "Up your ass, huh?"

Red fussed her cheeks, and she slapped my shoulder, scrambling to get back to her own feet.

I let her go, chuckling. "I'll give you whatever the hell you want, Jessie Blacke."

The damn longing in her eyes at my words made me want to promise her the world.

"Be back in a couple hours," I told her.

She kept silent while I shrugged on my coat, pulled on my hat and gloves, and headed for the door.

"I want fresh bear steaks for supper!" she hollered after me as I let in a blast of cold air.

"You got it." I shut myself out, squinting in the pristine white. The wind had blown hard enough to almost clear some areas of ground, while what looked like one to two-foot drifts covered others.

Ice crusted the river's banks, a hint of sun through clouds creating a picture any artist would love to paint. Beauty to the point of appearing fake.

I turned toward the mountains behind me, my heart full while eying the brush and trail I took northward into the hills.

The black bear had taken that route, a decent blood trail dripping amidst his tracks indenting the light snow. About two hundred yards along, he veered off the main path I'd forged over the summer. I kept a steady eye on my surroundings while taking it easy on my knee, ears straining for any sound beyond the cracking of twigs beneath my boots and the soft thumps of snow falling off branches.

Warmth thrummed through my body from the uphill hike, and I paced myself, cursing as the bit of sun we'd had slipped behind clouds. The bone-chilling cold burned my nostrils as I sucked in oxygen, the whiskers around my mouth coating with frost and ice.

The cold kept me alert, the thought of protecting Jessie and doing away with the latest threat bringing on a need beyond fear.

Snow began to fall again, not enough to cover the bear's tracks and blood splatters. Senses alert, I pushed onward, the rustle of branches in the growing wind overhead filling my ears.

27

JESSIE

Deciding I'd rather wait for Brock to give me an orgasm than my own fingers, I stoked the fire and grabbed his journal for some reading. He'd written in it every night I'd been with him, simply jotting a few notes from the day, he'd said, to keep track of his time. While he hadn't offered to let me read it, he never tucked it out of sight, leaving it on the shelf above the table.

Brock had started the journal on day one of his new life, I took note of on page one, and although he hadn't used my name, he mentioned a stubborn vixen with pilot skills unseen, with a rocking body and mouth he'd be dreaming about in the coming months.

Warmth filled me—emotional and physical.

"What are you doing to me, Brock?" I whispered in the stillness, the ache in my chest obvious my missing him—and he'd been gone all of ten or so minutes. Letting out a heavy sigh, I snuggled into his pillow and continued.

He noted the weather. Foraged food. The chickadee following him into the cabin one day he'd left the door open. His daily dip in the river to bathe, his excitement at seeing the first shoots rise in the enclosed garden beds. A few dreams of a sassy vixen filled the pages—vivid with descriptors, his own hand-written erotica that tightened my nipples and soaked between my thighs.

I missed him even more.

He didn't write for a handful of days, and the first line of the next installment, "I killed Griz", demolished my arousal. Brock wrote about his fear in detail, about the darkness that seemed to take ahold of his mind while staying awake for three days out of fear. In exhaustion, he feared he'd crossed the line of sanity. He detailed the lucky shot, the bear's death, and the carnage in their fight's wake.

Blood, guts, and gore. He'd taken a bite of the warm heart, enjoying it more than a sane man ought to. Staking out the hide, covered in blood…

Then the buzz of a plane engine, and his scramble to the river's edge, watching me like an angel in flight, coming to bring him out of the darkness. The same sense of need to conquer, claim, had filled him to the point of breaking, and he'd taken me like an animal on the river's shore.

My pussy spasmed once more while reliving the same memory, and I slipped my hand beneath his baggy sweats to find my core a slick mess.

Brock's chickadee chirped a few times but cut off as footfalls sounded outside the door. My breath caught, and I moaned. A quick roll from the bed, and I hurried to let him in, needing his hands, his mouth on me, his breath and scent filling my lungs. I wrenched the door open and blinked at the stooped man filling the doorway. A man I recognized. One I hadn't seen since the summer before.

"Shiv—"

His fist cut off my words, and I crumpled down into my own darkness.

———

Cold.

My teeth chattered, and I tried to curl and wrap my arms around myself. I jostled side to side, trying to bring focus to my eyes, full consciousness to my rattled brain. Swift movement… Scratching noises…

Like a sled over snow.

Darkness.

Chattering teeth, shivers wrecking my body and pounding my head.

Whimpers sounded in my ears.

Can't move.

Rhythmic movement calmed me, and I dreamed of Brock's dark eyes, the tenderness of his touch. The emotion in his gaze…

My temples throbbed. Throat ached for water.

Darkness pulled me under.

Brock.

Cold.

I blinked, but couldn't see anything but black, my head a mass of throbbing nerve endings. Couldn't move—wrapped up. Something heavy over my face…

So tired.

Giving up the need to focus, I relaxed into the movement, uncaring of why or where, just needing to escape the pain.

28

BROCK

I smelled fresh bear shit before I found his ass sprawled out beside a burrow. He still breathed, but one bullet stopped the labored rise and fall of his chest. My adrenaline had long eased, leaving me steady and in control, but the scent and sight of warm blood coating my hands while I sliced him from throat to belly stirred the darkness inside me.

Primal urges bared my teeth, and I enjoyed gutting the fucker far more than I should have. Satisfaction coursed through me, leaving me on a goddamn high I knew the best release for. Thoughts of Jessie, her warm mouth, her hot, tight pussy—her ass—fought for dominance in my head while I pulled the bears innards from their cavity, steam rising, warm blood melting the snow beneath the carcass.

I tore off a bite of its heart with my teeth, chewed the coppery flesh to mush, and swallowed it down with a growl, my instinctual *fuck you, bear—how you like them apples?* ringing in my ears.

My land. My wilderness.

I didn't bother with a clean skin, merely hacked my way up the insides of its legs, peeling from neck to thighs. Just enough of its pelt to act as a tied-up bag to carry the four quarters I decided to take.

Darkness coated the sky, and blood and fur my clothing before I finished and started back the way I'd come. Within minutes of heading down hill, I cursed not bringing along the sled to carry my burden. There'd been blood enough at the point where I'd shot him outside the cabin, I knew I'd be cleaning the bear before nightfall.

I hadn't planned on taking the meat, but only a fool let good flesh go to waste in the wilderness. The smoker could always be puffing away during the dead of winter.

At least I'd thought to grab my small travel pack with its headlamp I kept ready to go by the front door. I strapped the light to my forehead, lighting my way, and the snow had eased up, leaving my indented footprints easier to follow than I'd expected.

Within the hour, I headed down the path into my valley, thoughts of the warm fire and Jessie's smile keeping my steps light. Love for the wildness around me, the untamed, untouched land, lay heavy in my chest, but longing for her fought to overshadow those feelings.

Her acceptance rivaled my mom's. A good woman, driven to excel, empathetic, a woman who kept her promises, no matter the cost. Stubborn and honest to a fault.

My kind of woman.

The twitch in my dick let me know he agreed and wanted to keep her just as much as the rest of me did.

But would she stay?

And if she left, would I be willing to give up what I'd found in order for *her* to keep *me*? Given the chance, I knew she'd return home to accomplish what she'd set out to do with her family's business and name, and I loved her enough to let her go chase that dream.

Love.

"Yeah," I muttered into the wind, trudging through the brush leading to my cabin. "Fucking found her—and I'll let her go if that's what she needs."

The truth stabbed at my chest like a goddamn knife, and I almost wished the darkness, the instinct to claim would rise enough I could stay selfish. Chain her to my bed. Take care of her and never let her leave my side. Stay holed up in the back woods, off-grid, no distractions outside living life pulling us away from one another.

Lips in a thin line, I approached the cabin, my brow furrowing at the lack of light flickering through the front windows. I'd been gone most of the day.

Had she fallen asleep without stoking the fire?

I slid the sack off my shoulder, angling my body toward the right, my headlamp flashing across the snow.

Human tracks.

One set, coming and going—and dragging a sled behind.

"The fuck?" My heart rate exploded, and I kicked in the door. "Jessie!"

The cabin sat dark. Empty. No sound save for my panted breaths.

"Jessie!" I screamed, spinning back toward the outdoors, my feet taking me twenty or so yards down the path created by whoever the fuck had come knocking. "Goddamnit!"

I hurried back inside, my hands shaking like hell while trying flicking on the battery-operated lamp. Held aloft, the bright glow lit the cabin's interior.

My journal lay on the unmade bed.

Jessie's boots sat beside the front door.

Gone without a struggle, but not of her own volition if I had to guess. She wouldn't have gone without her boots.

Without leaving me a note. We'd come too far for her to take off like she'd done before—I had zero fucking doubt.

I'd made the decision to leave her…

I'd failed her.

Darkness ate at my periphery, and I gave into the roar rising in my chest shoving against guilt that wanted to rise. My bellow echoed through the valley, a sick calm taking over me as it faded in the snow and wind.

Hunt.

The word echoed in my head as I grabbed a few supplies, stuffing my pack full. I would find my woman and bring her back home, no matter the cost. Hunt whoever the fuck took her and make them pay for thinking they could touch what belonged to me.

"Kill," I whispered, once more heading out into the dark. I grabbed my own sled in the event she wouldn't be able to walk once I found her. My stride steady, I focused on getting Jessie back, uncaring of whatever carnage I might leave behind.

Animal. Man.

Both would fall beneath my knife, and I would show them who ruled my wilderness.

29

JESSIE

A shriek jolted me back to full consciousness.

Flickering flames in a blackened fireplace. The stench of old piss and rancid body odor in my nose. Another shriek and grappling behind me.

"I'll have her!" a man shouted.

Fists hitting flesh.

A whimper.

He spit and cursed. "Do as you're told an' care for the woman. Or I'll be takin' a strap to your ass afore fucking you raw."

The old man—Shiv.

He hit me.

Between my eyes ached, and I closed them, biting back a groan, wishing for my mind to shut down again and leave me in quiet darkness.

Shiv had shown up on Brock's stoop. Hit me. Dragged me to a cabin I'd seen twice the summer before he'd dropped me for Cort's delivery service.

"Fuckin' bastard," a young voice muttered, and a hand jerked me onto my back.

I gasped as my head explode with pain like knives in my eyes and realized my hands tied tight in front of me, ropes wrapped tight around my ankles.

Shiv's daughter bent over me, glaring, her blue eyes icy—and full of a hardness a young teen ought never to have in her glare.

"Says he's gonna have yer old, dried up cunt," she hissed down at me, her breath rotten like her front teeth, her dark hair a matted rat's nest. "Like I ain't good enough for his shriveled prick no more."

She pressed her fingertip against the side of my head, and I cried out, shying away from her.

"Hold fuckin still!" she yelled, kicking my thigh. "Need t' stop the bleedin' afore he comes back inside."

I clenched my teeth, trying not to think about the dirty rag she wiped my temple with, the germs, and infection sure to set in. "Why am I here?" I managed through my teeth.

"Dunno. Guess my cunt ain't good enough no more. He had to go find *you*. Whore he couldn't keep his eyes offa last year." She snorted and stopped with the cleanup.

I cracked an eyelid to see her still glaring over me.

"You ain't gonna give him no baby. Shiv is mine. His prick is mine." She grabbed at her crotch beneath the sack-like dress she wore, her grin revealing two dark spaces where teeth ought to be. "I gots the tightest cunt, he says. His favorite little juicy hole."

The door opened, letting in cold air to shiver my skin.

"He wants t' use you," she hissed, her voice lowered, "but I ain't gonna let him."

"The fuck you talkin' 'bout, Linny girl?" Shiv snarled, his backhand shooting in my periphery to clobber the side of her face.

She clutched at her cheek, head downcast. "You're mine

and I'm yours. Just telling' this here whore how things go 'round here." Her mutter held a bite to it—Linny was not the submissive, cowed girl she appeared to be.

"How things go 'round here?" He huffed a snort and toed my ass. "Get up, woman. Had a hard enough time draggin' yer ass back over the mountain. Ain't gonna be totin' ya 'round no more. Gonna earn yer keep while yer here, that's for damn sure. Warmin' my bed, too."

"No!" His daughter shrieked and flew at him, scratching at his face and trying to knee him in the balls.

I closed my eyes against the sick sight, the pain, praying for darkness to spirit me away again.

Brock... Need you.

30

BROCK

R age kept me warm.

The need to spill blood gave me energy through the night, numbed me to the pain in my knee.

Hours passed, my focus on the bobbing headlight revealing the path I followed, heading through the pass Jessie had told me about.

Shiv.

I had no fucking doubt. Sick fuck had taken my woman, dragged her over the ridge and down through the pass.

I should have ended him when he'd shown up months earlier. Should have sliced him from throat to groin. Gutted him and left his innards for the bears. Should have chopped off his dick. His legs and arms. Sliced out his tongue for talking the way he'd done.

Fucking his daughter. Offering her every hole to a stranger. Wanting my sperm to give her a baby.

Red filled my vision, the lust for blood thrumming through my body.

No fear.

Pure adrenaline high—with deadly calm.

Night faded, and still I strode onward, my sled tied around my waist and trailing along behind me, the wind buffeting me all night and drifting snow over Shiv's tracks in places. Twice, I'd had to backtrack to find his trail.

The scent of woodsmoke wafted past me, and I slowed my steps through the woods, wondering if my exhausted mind played tricks on me. A slight rise ahead hopefully promised a good view, and I climbed, my breaths the only sound in the white stillness around me.

I crawled up the final few feet to the hill's top, peeking my head over, searching through the trees on the slight decline ahead.

More woodsmoke… A dark tendril slid into the late morning sky, and I followed it downward, scooting toward my right to better see through the trees.

There.

Small cabin. Sagging roof. A sled propped up beside the front door.

My heart rate stilled even as adrenaline pulled me from my body's exhaustion. I clutched the darkness close in my mind, letting instinct guide me as I crept through the trees, my focus honed in like a stalking lion sneaking up on its prey. Four hundred yards. Three hundred.

I stopped behind a patch of briars, untying my sled from my waist while studying the cabin.

No sound emanated. No movement around the gray, log walls or through the lone window on its front.

Crouching down regardless of the ache growing in my knee, I pulled my binoculars from my pack and took a closer look, my breath fogging in the still cold air. It'd warmed at least ten degrees since the sky lightened, but it hovered close to freezing. At least the snow hadn't continued to fall.

No movement whatsoever.

I had no qualms ending Shiv for what he'd done—but what about his daughter? She'd been abused, but enough she'd keep quiet about what I was about to do? Would she want to go back with us? Catch a flight out and find whatever family she might have outside of the wilderness?

Remembering all I'd endured, the media, the lies... I couldn't stomach the not knowing if she would keep her mouth shut or not.

Kill.

The darkness demanded I let no one threaten me or my woman. That meant ending Shiv's daughter, too.

I pushed against the humanity quaking at the thought of ending an innocent girl's life. But I would do whatever it took to keep Jessie safe—even if it meant leaving carnage in my wake.

A shadow passed the window. Life inside.

And I would bring death.

31

JESSIE

My body ached, but my memory served me well in reminding me where I lay when I came to—I managed to bite back a groan and take stock of my situation without moving to let Shiv and Linny know I woke.

Still bound, I rested in an unchanged cabin except for the weak sunlight in the front window.

I lay on my back on the hard, dirt floor by the fire. The throbbing in my head had lessened somewhat, enough I didn't struggle to focus on my surroundings.

Linny sat cross-legged beside me, her gaze on the snorting lump atop the lone bed against the far wall, a huge buck knife in her hand. The low fire on my other side lit half of her face, highlighting the beginnings of a bruise on her cheekbone that hadn't been there earlier. Dried blood crusted beneath her nose. The neck of her dress torn and gaping to reveal her small breast—and scars that looked like knife slashes across her chest.

Steady breaths escaped her parted lips.

Fear clawed at my mind as my dire situation fell fully on

my mind. Shiv had rattled my brain again, and I lay close to helpless, at his mercy. At the mercy of the feral young woman sitting still as a stone beside me. Holding a damn knife that could gut me with a few flicks of her wrist.

A snort sounded, and Shiv shifted beneath the blankets.

"Not gonna let him fuck you," his daughter whispered, switching the knife over to her right hand.

Maybe assurance of my being on her side would help my dire situation. Women bonding together and all that shit even though Linny was the last female on earth I'd want as a friend.

"I don't want him," I whispered back past the dryness and pulse throbbing in my throat "He belongs to you. He's your man."

"Damn right," she growled.

"Did he hurt you?"

She glanced down at me, and my mouth gaped open at the cuts across the other side of her face, the dried blood that had dripped from the wounds. "He likes t' cut me with this here knife." She held it aloft, her wild eyes glinting in the fire as she caressed the blade with her gaze. "Gets his prick hard so he can fuck me. Couldn't get it up after we fought last night, though. And my cunt was drippin' to be filled."

Fuck. I clenched my eyes shut, fighting to keep calm, keep my heart rate from jacking to high fucking heaven. *Brock...*

He must have returned already to find me gone from the cabin, but how much snow had fallen? Would there be tracks left for him to follow? If not, would he even think to head over the mountain in search of me? Had he even met Shiv or knew where he lived?

"Says he's gonna have you come sunrise when he's rested

from haulin' yer ass through the pass, but I ain't gonna let him."

Curses rang in my head. The fuck could I do? Aching and far from my usual strength, I wracked my mind for a way out of my situation, knowing I couldn't rely on Brock. Physically, I didn't have a chance, bound as I was. Even without the ropes, I doubted I could stand on my own, let alone grapple with the feisty young woman watching over me.

Feisty and young—probably strong for her age considering where she'd grown up and how she'd lived her life.

And Shiv… His back stooped, but he still had power behind his punch. He'd dragged me on what must have been a sled all the way from Brock's cabin. Just shy of ten miles. In snow. Rugged terrain.

Shiv was the danger—not his daughter. But combined, they would prove a mountain I had no chance of scaling.

I eyed the bed. Considered the knife in the girl's hand and decided I really didn't have any other choice than to go with what I'd started.

"You're a brave woman," I whispered, forcing myself to hold her gaze as she once more turned toward me. "Beautiful and strong."

She blinked, a hint of a frown flickering over her brow.

"Shiv should treat you like the queen you are—you take care of him, right?"

Her chin lifted. "Everything I do is for him."

"Cook and clean?"

"I do all the household chores, even suck the shriveled prick so he can give me a baby," she said, glancing over at his sleeping form.

A shiver wracked through me. "And this is how he repays you? Bringing another woman to your home, your castle, threatening to have his way with her?"

A low growl rose in her chest, and she hunched forward. "I ain't suckin' his prick to get it hard for *you*." She spit on the floor.

"How could he even ask you to do such a thing?" I forced out, bile rising. "Everything you do for him, and he treats you like dirt."

Silence reigned, and I waited. Praying like hell her little mind would sway her in the way I wanted.

"You deserve so much more," I whispered. "Love. Affection without the pain."

"I like the pain. Makes my cunt wet."

Shit.

She glanced down at me again. "But Shiv says we need the money, so I gotta keep my mouth shut and do as I'm told, or he won't cut me no more."

Money... The fuck?

"I have money," I told her, my shaking voice giving away my rising panic. "Lots of it. You cut me loose, help me get out of here, and I'll help you find a better man. A man who can give you pain without scaring up your beautiful body. A good man who—"

Shiv grunted and rolled, his eyes opening, gaze landing on the two of us, snagging the breath clear out of my lungs. "Come here, Linny girl."

His daughter didn't move, and I held my breath as he shoved the ratty blankets to his knees, revealing his wrinkled nakedness. "Come here," he repeated, palming his semi-hard dick, tugging on it a few times.

Still, Linny sat unmoving beside me, and I glanced between the two as they stared at one another.

"Want yer warm mouth. Yer sweet, juicy cunt," Shiv said, and I gagged at the bile rising up the back of my throat. "You give me yers," he warned, his tone low, "or I'll be havin' hers instead. Make you sit on her pretty face. Let her lick yer cream while I fuck her raw."

A low whine built in the girl's chest, and she shot up, rushing the bed.

Shiv caught her forearm as she raised to slash the knife at him, and I struggled to push to an elbow and scoot away, whimpering, biting back sobs as they grappled over the knife.

Linny shrieked and clawed like a feral animal, but he held her wrist in a vice grip, his silence more terrifying than her wildness. "I deserve to be treated like a queen!" she screamed, yanking in his hold. "I deserve more than yer fists! Yer limp prick! I want a baby! And you can't even get it up to gi—"

He punched out with their clasped hands, sinking the knife into her throat, cutting off her words.

Time slowed to a crawl as blood poured, soaking the front of him and her alike, their stares locked on one another.

My bladder released with a rush as I gaped, unblinking. Processing. Thoughts scattered.

Shiv's daughter slumped over him, but he pushed her away, taking the knife from her neck. He swung his legs off the bed and stood as her body slid to the floor with a soft thump. Eyes dead as his daughter's turned my way. Lust parted his lips amidst the blood-splattered beard lining his jawline.

Blood covered his torso. Dripped down over his paunched gut. Dripped onto his stiff dick.

Oh, fuck. Fuck. Fuck.

He stalked my way, knife in hand, and I scrambled backward, sobbing through the pain in my head. Helpless. Hopeless.

"You might have a dried-out cunt," he said, his tone void of emotion, same as his eyes, "but Linny's blood gonna make it easy to fuck you."

32

BROCK

I stalked forward, my footfalls near silent in the fluffy snow, my knife in hand. While I didn't remember drawing it from the scabbard on my hip, I took comfort in its weight, the darkness having decided to end life slowly rather than with a bullet that could be traced.

Once I saved Jessie, I would torch the fucking place. Leave no physical evidence of what went down. Nothing to lead authorities to me.

No one would be out to the wilderness for months if I were lucky. No one would know Shiv and his blood—daughter included—had spilled beneath my hand.

Less than two hundred yards lay between me and my prey. My mouth watered to taste blood, my mind buzzed from lack of sleep, adrenaline keeping me upright.

Jessie.

Mine.

The buzzing intensified in my ears, and I slowed, shaking my head and blinking.

The cabin sat unmoved, focused in my line of sight—but the buzzing grew louder.

Plane.

My conscious took note, dragging my gaze to the sky.

No.

Heart rate jacking, I scanned overhead, my plans shredded to fuck. Growling, I squatted down, hoping for a mere fly-over, biting back a muffled curse over my goddamn knee tweaking from the cold and overuse.

The sound of the engine roared, crawling up my backside, and I turned, peering through the trees behind me.

A small plane on skis dipped in low, bringing another growl up from my chest.

He circled Shiv's, and although no wording plastered along its metal sides, my gut settled on truth I knew as solidly as the knife in my hand.

Trouble. A shit fucking ton of trouble.

33

JESSIE

Shiv stood over me, jacking his blood-covered dick with one hand, the knife dripping in the other held at his side.

Fighting to keep oxygen in my lungs, I glanced over at Linny's lifeless form, her eyes open and glazed, blood a pool around her head on the dirt floor. I couldn't scramble back far enough—a wall stopped me, and I whimpered, jerking my focus back to Shiv.

"My Linny girl is gone. Think I'll be keeping' you in her place. Fuck the money. Fuck *him*. Yer mine now."

Money. Him.

Shiv approached, lifting his knife and cutting off my speeding thoughts.

"Please," whimpered, tucking my knees beneath me, making myself as small as possible. "Please…"

"Beggin' for my dick?" He held it by the base, pointing it toward me.

Bile rose, and I gagged, clenching my eyes shut and shaking my head.

"Blood's dryin'. Open up that pretty mouth and make me good and wet for you, Jessie, girl."

I gagged again, sitting back to lean against the wall as his stench filled my nose along with my own piss wetting Brock's sweatpants.

Metal pressed against my neck, and I stilled, breath once more held, rather than try to fight him off with my tied hands.

"Open yer mouth—and if I feel a mere graze of teeth on my prick, this here blade will send hot blood gushing from your veins, too."

Thoughts of Brock kept me from desiring death.

Suck his dick—take it in my body if need be—but live another day.

Survive.

Find a way to make Shiv pay, find a way to make it back to Brock.

Hot flesh smacked against my lips, and I swallowed another gag at the rancid musk of Shiv and the copper scent filling my nose.

"Open," he growled, the knife stinging my neck.

Tears rolled from beneath my clenched eyelids.

Brock.

"Now!" Shiv hissed, pressing the knife hard enough wet heat slid down my throat.

Whimpering, I did as told, unclenching my jaw and parting my lips.

He shoved forward, his dick not long enough to gag me, but the taste, the putrid scent of unwashed body…

I gagged, and he groaned, pulled out, and shoved back in as I pressed my bound hands against his thigh, trying to force him away.

"So hot and wet," Shiv groaned, thrusting again.

Bile erupted, spewing around his length to dribble down my chin, but he kept his groin against my face, trapping my head against the wall while I gagged and struggled to breathe, my fingernails clawing at his thighs.

The sick fuck didn't even care I'd puked around his dick —he kept up his short thrusts, his grunts and groans wracking my body with dry heaves.

Shiv groaned something about me being a good girl, the knife's bite disappearing from my neck's tender flesh.

I grabbed his balls and yanked.

He let out a shriek, ripping away from me.

My eyelids snapped up, and I tensed, ready for his doubled over form to launch my way.

He'd dropped the blade and clutched his sack I'd tried to rip from his body. "Fuckin' cunt!" He groaned, stumbling back another stop. "Gonna fuckin' kill you. Gut you."

An engine roared overhead—plane.

I scooted toward the door with a cry, and Shiv hollered, grabbing his knife again, even though he still bent over, one hand on his balls.

"Don't. Fuckin'. Move." He spit each word, the blade's tip still red from Linny's blood drawing me up short.

Plane.

Money.

Shiv spun and kicked one of the chairs, slamming it into the wall. "Fuck!"

I hunkered down again, wiping my mouth against Brock's sweatshirt. Need to spit the lingering flavor of Shiv and puke from my mouth, but I didn't want to draw his attention.

Still cursing, he yanked on pants as the obvious sound of a plane engine once more approaching and landing on the strip Shiv kept cleared for deliveries. He yanked on boots. Shirt. Coat—left gaping open.

Eyes dead, he approached with a rag in hand. "Open up."

I did as told, and he stuffed my mouth full, using another rag to bind it in place behind my head.

"Stay put, or I'll tie yer ass to my bed and take yer puckered hole without anything but my spit."

I jerked my head in agreement, and he flung open the door, stepped out into the cold, and slammed it shut behind him. Tears poured down my cheeks as I fought to breathe through the stench of the rag he'd shoved in my mouth. It smelled like shit and tasted even worse.

The plane engine cut out, and I stilled again, my nostrils flared from trying to draw clean oxygen into my lungs.

Silence rang in my ears, and I glanced over at Linny.

I slept. Had to.

Nightmare, I whispered to myself, clenching my eyes shut again. Swallowing a dry as hell sob let me know I lived it— wide awake and conscious.

Helpless.

Sobs wracked me, and I struggled to calm myself. Find my own two feet to stand on. Where had my strength gone? Where had my drive to succeed fly off to?

Brock...

Steps approached. Voices.

The door swung in, and I whimpered again as Shiv strode in—with Cort Endsley on his heels.

34

BROCK

I stared hard at the man who hopped out of the cockpit. Not anyone I recognized.

Shiv remained by the cabin, watching the man approach.

No sound came from inside. No scream for help.

If alive and conscious, Jessie would have heard the plane. She'd be fighting like a goddamn Tasmanian devil to escape.

The idea she might be dead tore my guts to shreds, but I stayed put. Trying to evaluate the situation in my exhausted brain.

"Cort." Shiv's voice reached me through the still air.

Cort.

Fucking Cort Endsley.

They shook hands, and everything clicked into place in my head. My rage returned, bringing back the blood lust to overshadow my grief in thinking she might already be gone.

I stood and silently hurried toward them, too far gone in my need to kill to make a sound.

The men turned and moved into the cabin, leaving the door gaping—and I sprinted forward, my chest tight as fuck. Heart pounding.

No exhaustion touched me as I honed in on bloodshed.

Snow kicking up beneath my feet. Arms and pulse pumping.

Fucking red…

My bum leg twisted, and I went down hard, pain tearing through my knee.

"Fuck!" I ground through clenched teeth, grabbing at my knee, knife lost in the snow beside me. "Fuck!"

I scrambled to stand, but my knee put me back down. Growling, I thrashed in the snow, finding my knife, and dragged my ass forward on hands and one knee, snow finding its way beneath my gloves' band, cold on my heated skin.

A muffled shriek sounded from inside.

Jessie.

Alive. Scared. Because of me.

Teeth clenched against the pain, I stood and managed a few hobbled steps before face planting again.

I can't protect her.

Can't save her.

Guilt and hopelessness swooped in like a nor'easter, freezing my mind, my limbs.

The rage faded, leaving me wracked in pain.

Act, or she dies.

I couldn't give up.

Wouldn't.

Groaning, I crawled forward on my good leg, jaw clenched against the one dragging behind, my gaze focused on the open doorway and the muffled voices from inside.

35

JESSIE

Cort scanned the cabin's interior, his eyes hard, nostrils flaring, as he took in Linny's body. "The fuck?" He muttered. His lips parted from their thin line as his gaze jerked my way. "What the *fuck*?" he repeated, shoving Shiv out of his way to get to me. "I told you not to hurt her!"

He dropped to his knees beside me, seemingly uncaring of the piss and puke on me.

I pressed against the wall, leaning away from his reaching hands, his words filtering through my brain.

He'd told Shiv not to hurt me.

Money.

Whimpering, I turned away, but Cort untied the rag from around my head, yanking the gag from my mouth.

I let out a shriek and punched at him with my bound hands, but he clasped my forearm.

"I warned you, Jessie, but you couldn't listen. Why couldn't you just let me have what I wanted, hmm?" He smoothed back my hair off my forehead, that crazy in his eyes I'd seen hints of before filling his orbs as he tracked his focus down over my face. "And now it's come to this. Me having to dish out even more money to get what I want."

"You can't have her."

Shiv's declaration yanked Cort's head around. "She's mine."

"I need someone now with my Linny girl gone. Need a woman out here. Pussy." Shiv eyed me, lust in his gaze.

"You can't have her," Cort repeated at Shiv through clenched teeth, turning back toward me, a sick tenderness in his gaze.

"Just once. Her ass. Let me have that hole—just once."

He'd fucking lost it. Knifed his daughter, and still covered in her blood, begged to shove his dick up my ass.

"No," Cort barked. "I brought your payment. That's all you're getting. That mess isn't my problem," he said pointing at Linny's body. "Same as your wife's wasn't. I'm done with you, Shiv. You take the money and forget all about this." Cort dug an envelope from beneath his coat and tossed it toward Shiv.

The old man caught it, clutching it to his chest.

Cort turned toward me once more, and I shivered beneath his perusal. "So much like him," he whispered, rubbing his thumb over my lower lip. "His eyes. His fire."

My dad...

"He refused me, same as you, but unlike him, you refuse to die, to let me go. And so, it's come to this."

He'd sabotaged my plane.

Cold air swept from the open door, raising goose bumps over my skin, as my mind tried to connect dots I couldn't quite make out.

"You killed my parents, didn't you?" I asked, my voice barely a rasp.

A sad smile lifted his lips. "I'd like to say it was in a fit of impassioned rage, but tampering with a car with the intent to harm is premeditated, wouldn't you say?"

My breath snagged.

"But you." Cort rubbed my lower lip again. "You…"

Shiv ghosted up behind Cort, his arm and knife raising.

My body reacted, my focus jerking to his face.

Cort spun, and the two men collided.

I scrambled for the door, sobbing, as furniture crashed behind me. Light sky—freedom beckoned. Another blast of cold air.

A hand grasped my ankle and dragged me back.

"No!" I shrieked, twisting and thrashing my bound arms.

Cort.

Shiv lay alongside Linny, the knife sticking out of his eye.

I heaved and sobbed, scrambling to get away, but Cort climbed atop me, holding my arms overhead.

"Shh." Minty fresh breath fanned over my face, and I bit my lip, turning my head to the side, eyes clenched tight while trying to buck him off me. "I'm going to take what I want, then end you like I did your father for all the heartache he caused. Wish to fuck I'd been able to off you when you were a kid, but even then, I wanted you like I'd wanted him."

I stilled at his words, and he licked the tear leaking down my cheek.

"My friend."

He licked along my lips.

"My lover."

Bile burned my throat. He and my father… I swallowed hard, refusing to believe the shit spewing from his mouth.

"Why?" I heard myself whisper. "W-why hurt him if you loved him?"

"Because he loved his wife more." Cort nosed along my jaw, his breath a hot brand. "Because she refused to share a

second time, and he wouldn't give me what I wanted
without her with us. She couldn't be bought. Neither
could he."

And neither could I.

A shudder rippled through me as he tongued my ear, and
he groaned, misreading my body's reaction. He ground
against my core, and the truth of his arousal sent another
shudder through me.

"Sweet, sweet Jessie," he whispered, his lips finding mine
for a gentle swipe, his hard dick pressing against my thigh.
"At least I'm not a sick pedophilic like Shiv—I waited for
you to grow up."

I lay lax, hopeless and helpless as he brushed his mouth
over mine, probing with his tongue.

"So beautiful, so goddamn delicious," he groaned. "Just
like your father."

Let the stupid fuck in…

Going on instinct as I'd done with Linny, I gave him my
tongue in return, fighting off the need to gag while moaning.

Let him think he'd swayed me. Let him think I
wanted him.

"You saved me," I whispered the second he let me
breathe, lifting my hips to keep in contact with his dick.

He groaned again, grinding against me, his tongue
seeking out ever recess in my mouth.

"Untie me, Cort. Let me touch you," I whispered between
kisses.

With a muttered curse, he pulled away, leaving me chilled
through as he yanked his knife from Shiv's eye.

I held my bound hands upward, and Shiv's blood dripped
onto my chin as Cort sliced through the rope.

"My feet," I whispered. "I need to wrap my legs around
you—please. Let me give you what my dad wouldn't, what

my cunt of a mother refused you." My throat burned, but I held Cort's gaze.

I would stand on my own two feet. I would defeat him…

The second the ropes fell from my ankles, I kicked out at his crouched form beside me, sending him tumbling onto his back.

I scrambled for the door, adrenaline getting my feet beneath me.

Something bashed against my head, and I fell forward, my fingertips inches from the doorway. Pain radiated down my neck, and I gasped, fighting off the darkness creeping in my periphery while clawing for the outdoors.

No. Please, no…

Cort yanked me fully into the cabin and flipped me onto my back, keeping me conscious. "Lying bitch!" He smacked me across the face, and I blinked in hazy pain, barely aware he pulled Brock's sweats from my legs. "I told you I always get what I want. You wouldn't give it to me willingly, and now I've destroyed everything you value. I'll have you—then end you just like I promised."

I blinked his hazy form above me into focus.

He shoved down his jeans, palming his hard dick. "Don't even care you pissed yourself and stink like an outhouse. Going to own this cunt."

He kicked my useless legs apart and knelt between my thighs, jacking his dick, swiping the head up over my slit. "Mine."

I belong to Brock…

The truth rose inside me along with a rush of adrenaline, giving me clarity of mind and a sudden burst of energy regardless of my throbbing temples. I fought. Scratched and kicked. Screamed and bit, a feral bitch hellbent on saving herself.

36

BROCK

J essie's shriek pulled me to my feet, and I clenched my teeth against the pain, stumbling toward the cabin's open door, knife in a death grip in my freezing hand.

Need to protect her. Save her.

One agonizing step. Another. Steadily forward, but not nearly fucking fast enough.

Goddamnit! I'm coming… Please don't fucking hurt her!

Her hands appeared in the doorway, clawing for the daylight—she ripped from my sight.

"Lying bitch!" a man hollered—too young a voice to be Shiv.

Fucking Cort. He muttered some more, too low for me to make out.

"Jessie," I whispered, knowing I needed to keep silent. Use stealth since physically, both Shiv and Cort would be able to take me. Five steps.

"Don't even care you pissed yourself and stink like an outhouse," Cort said, his voice reaching me. "Going to own this cunt."

Four. A growl rumbled in my chest. Three.

"Mine," he said with a grunt—and all hell broke loose inside. Shrieking like a goddamn cat, Cort's bellows.

My sassy vixen putting up a fight. Two.

One.

A feral grin lifted my lips, and I pulled myself up to stand on the threshold.

Cort rutted between my woman's thighs as she kicked her socked feet against his calves, her head thrashing as he tried to eat at her mouth.

"ARG!" I bellowed and swung my blade while rushing forward in a haze of adrenaline, slashing up across Cort's cheek, my other fist shooting out to knock him back onto his ass, his dick hard—and dry. Blood lust dragged me forward as he fought to keep conscious. It didn't appear like he'd dipped into my woman, but that truth didn't offer me peace.

Awareness of unmoving bodies beyond him registered, but all I could focus on was Cort Endsley, the man who thought he could own what belonged to me. The man probably responsible for Jessie's heartache of losing her parents. The man who'd stalked and haunted her. The man who'd driven her to drink, to stress, to fear.

She'd fought him off.

"And now it's my turn to protect what's mine," I growled down at him.

He groaned and tried to roll, but I grasped his flagging dick and sliced clean through with one quick slash.

A rushed intake of air, and he screamed like a woman, blood leaking from his groin.

"Brock."

Jessie's whisper ripped my focus off Cort.

She pushed to stand on shaking feet, her hand outstretched. Face blank, her attention on the writhing man at my feet, she gestured with her hand. "Give it to me."

Wooden voice. Calm.

In shock.

My sweatshirt covered her upper body, falling long enough to caress her upper, bare thighs.

"Jessie." Her name ripped ragged from my throat.

"Give me the knife, Brock."

I handed it over, my adrenaline waning, hands starting to shake.

She grasped the hilt with white knuckles and climbed onto Cort's chest as he clutched at his oozing groin. "See this?" she hissed, lifting my sweatshirt, baring her pussy to him. "This will never belong to you. *Never*." She dropped the sweatshirt and stabbed him in the shoulder.

He bucked, and I fell onto his legs to keep him still for her to exact revenge.

"That's for my mom," she grunted, wrenching the knife free.

Another stab to his other shoulder as he squirmed beneath her thighs clutching his arms against his body.

"For Dad." A sob ripped from her lips.

"Jessie," he groaned. "Please, baby—"

"Not."

Stab.

"Your."

Stab.

"Baby."

Both hands on the hilt, she raised it high—and slammed it home into Cort's eye with a gut-wrenching scream.

His legs stopped thrashing.

Jessie's heavy breaths filled my ears, and I reached for her shoulder.

She shied away from me with a shriek, the blade lifting.

"It's me," I murmured, holding up my hands and backing off Cort's legs. "It's Brock. Your Brock."

She blinked, the knife lowering to her lap.

"Jessie?"

"I-I killed him."

"We both did."

She glanced at Cort. Turned her head to take in Shiv and the young woman who must be his daughter, her neck slashed to shit.

Jessie crawled to Shiv's side, picked up the old man's blade, wiped it down, and wrapped Cort's hand around it.

"N-need to get the ropes h-he bound me with," she whispered, rising to her feet and swaying. "Your sweatpants… Need to clean up my piss…"

I stood and yanked Jessie into my arms.

The knife thumped to the cabin's dirt floor, and she sobbed, clinging to me.

"I got you, vixen. Never fucking letting you go."

37

JESSIE

Since I expected Cort hadn't told anyone where he'd flown off to, I knew we had time before anyone came looking for him.

Leaving the bodies lay where they'd fallen, Brock and I took time to build up the fire and rest, the carnage unavoidable, but neither of us felt well enough to trek the ten miles back to his cabin. Refusing to think on what I'd done—what could have happened if Brock hadn't shown up when he did, I poked through the cabin's contents, avoiding looking at the carnage around us.

A trunk at the foot of the blood-soaked bed held worn woman's clothing. I pulled on a pair of pants and thicker socks. Old boots that must have belonged to Shiv's wife lay at the bottom and fit my feet a bit snug, but better than nothing.

While I'd have preferred to not eat anything from the cabin that stank of rancid body odor and blood, I needed sustenance, same as Brock. Canned goods still in date provided what we needed, and I forced down the tuna and beans.

"Going to burn this place to the ground," Brock said, breaking the silence that had hung like a death shroud over us, tossing the cans into the fireplace.

I nodded my agreement and helped him lay out broken furniture and blankets in a path from the fire around the cabin's interior—fuel to feed the flames. Once finished, he lit a tattered book on fire, and held it aloft until flames licked high, before tossing it onto the bed where the ticking he'd ripped open in the dry corner offered dried grass, the perfect fire starter.

Smoke and flames rose, and without another word, we slipped out the front door, both of us battered and bruised. Moving slowly through the cold air, I tucked my body tucked beneath his shoulder, helping to keep weight off his knee.

The crackling of a raging fire reached us before we'd gone deep enough into the woods to pass from sight. I refused to turn back to watch. I refused to think on anything other than the too-long trek ahead and the cabin awaiting us.

We reached his sled, and once he fashioned a crutch to replace me beneath his arm, I took the sled's rope in hand, dragging it behind my slow steps, the weight of his pack and the extra canned goods we'd taken proving to be almost too much weight for my exhausted, battered body.

A mere mile lay behind us—and snow started to fall.

My throat tightened, but I refused the tears to fall. I was strong. Brock was a beast. Nothing and no one would keep us down. Cold air bit at my face with every slow drag of my feet. The old boots didn't offer proper insulation, I counted myself lucky it wasn't January with sub-zero temperatures that would promise frostbite. Still, the ache from being chilled through heightened my exhaustion until I plodded on in a foggy haze of white, following the hunched man ahead of me doing the same.

We made it maybe halfway up the pass before Brock pulled up short. "Need to stop for the night."

Darkness didn't yet coat the sky overhead, but enough snow fell to block out most of whatever daylight we had left.

"Not going to find much better than that," he said, pointing to a low overhang of rock that would offer a bit of shelter. "I'll gather pine boughs if you can start a fire."

The thought of a warm fire and laying down brought tears of relief to my eyes, but I blinked them back, slowly dragging the sled up to the overhang. While the rock wouldn't allow us to stand beneath it, the dry ground stretched back close to five feet, and curved off to the right—away from what little wind did blow. The small cave-like area offering a perfect sized place for us to rest. I finally released my cramped hand from its rope burden to dig through his pack.

I built a teepee with dried branches in front of where Brock began laying fresh-cut boughs toward the overhang's back, using stuffing from the old coat's frayed bottom and waterproof matches from his pack to light it. Thankful as hell the snow that the fallen snow had been light and not heavy, wet flakes, I continued to feed the small fire dead branches I'd snapped off the pine trees around us until a nice, warm fire crackled, its heat trapping in our hideaway behind me.

The wind died down fully, but the snow continued to fall.

Together, we dragged a few bigger pieces of wood beneath the rock, not nearly enough to see us through the night, but enough to give us a few hours of warmth to sleep.

"Should one of us keep watch?" I asked when he finally sat on our bough bed, his back against the rock wall, his face white, the winter cap he had pulled over his ears brushing the overhang's ceiling.

"Nothing moving out there in this. Come lay down."

"Want something to eat?" I reached for his pack.

"No. Just sleep." He slumped to his side with a heavy sigh, and I moved to curl up in front of him, facing the fire. "I want you behind me," he said with a grunt, pulling me up and over his body, my back close to the wall.

"Not as warm back here," I grumbled.

"But safer," he argued, settling his body around mine in a protective shield. "Gotta keep you safe," he murmured and fell silent.

Tiredness weighed me into the boughs, and I welcomed the darkness I'd been fighting for hours. Sleep, peaceful and quiet, slipped in.

38

BROCK

Our silence carried on through the next day as we struggled against the snow. Jessie fared better than me, the rest and food giving her the energy to move. My goddamn knee and the cold kept me clutching the crutch I'd made. Took most of the day, but we reached home before twilight replaced the weak sun's rays.

I started the wood stove and heated water.

Jessie started a fire in the fireplace and heated up canned stew for our dinner after burning the ropes, clothes, and boots she'd taken from Shiv's cabin.

We hadn't spoken of what had happened and had hiked most of the day keeping our thoughts to ourselves.

Hunger to know the truth, what had happened in detail, ate at my stomach until it burned, and no food or water eased its unrest.

Had Shiv touched her?

Cort's dick hadn't looked like it'd been inside my woman, but the way he'd rutted against her…

Teeth clenched, I took a sponge bath with in a bucket of hot water, trying to ignore the fact Jessie did the same behind me, warmer by the fire, erasing the final bits of evidence to link us to Shiv's homestead. Unable to keep from checking I didn't dream, that she'd returned with me, I glanced her way.

She'd stripped naked, her back toward me, and I studied every inch of her skin, looking for bruising, signs of abuse while dropping my rag into my bucket of tepid, dirtied water.

I'd thought I'd lost her, and while I hadn't, I wondered if I'd truly saved her in time—

She bent, baring her backside, a peek of her pussy between her thighs as she wiped down her shins.

Sudden lust to take her, fill her with my scent, my cum, raged through me, and I fisted my hands at my sides, my dick swelling.

"Did either of those fuckers touch you?" I rasped through grit teeth, the need to know overriding my patience for her to talk when she was ready.

Slowly, Jessie straightened and turned, no trace of sass or my vixen in her stare as her gaze flickered down to my raging hard on I didn't bother trying to hide. I held my breath— fucking waiting for her face to pale out of fear, for her to shy away from my obvious want.

"I wasn't raped," she whispered, her attention lifting to my face, a slew of emotion rising in her eyes to bridge the gap between us.

My breath left in a rush, and I hobbled toward her, hands fisted at my sides, so far gone in my lust, I didn't feel the pain in my knee. I stood close enough she had to tip her head back to hold my gaze, my entire body trembling. "He rutted between your thighs," I forced out words to the memory replaying in my head.

"Trying to get it up." Jessie rested her hand on my chest, her touch searing clear through to my heart, her lips parting at the rapid thumps beating beneath her palm.

"I'm barely hold on, Jessie," I said, my voice a ragged whisper. "Feel like a fucking feral animal. Need—" I choked back the words, fighting the urge to be a selfish prick.

Jessie took one of my hands, pried my fingers open, and pressed my palm to her breast. "Erase their memory," she whispered, her shaking voice tempting the rage for blood to rise.

Instead, I cupped her heavy breast, gently squeezing and studying her face for any sign of fear or hesitation, my thread of restraint near snapping.

She sighed and leaned into my touch. "More."

"Jessie…" I groaned while palming her other breast, my mouth salivating, my dick leaking a bead of pre-cum down my jutting length.

"Please," she whimpered, her eyes wide and welling as I rolled both nipples between my fingers. "Need you. Fill me up—make it all go away."

My dick jerked between us, and with a growl, I swept her up into my arms, stumbling the three feet to my bed to gently lay her down even as every cell in my body screamed to claim with haste. Pound my dick into her body until she screamed my name, until I coated her insides with my cum, and pulled out to shove my seed back in with my fingers.

I lay half atop her, buried my face in her neck, fighting like fuck for calm, my hips grinding my dick against her thigh. Breaths ragged. Mind at war with my body.

"Brock." She smoothed her fingers through my hair.

"Just … give me a minute." I trembled beneath her touch, hanging onto restraint with a failing grasp.

"I'm okay, Brock," she whispered against my ear. "I'm okay."

I lifted onto my elbow, studying her eyes. Wetness coated

them, but the need shining through the tears choked my own throat.

"I'm okay," she repeated, her hands gently cupping my bearded cheeks. "I want you to take me." She spread her thighs wide. "Feel me—feel how wet I am for you."

Fuck.

I ran my shaking hand over the downy hair atop her mound, my fingers finding wetness seeping from her soft petal-like lips. A groan rumbled my chest.

"Let go—"

I slammed my mouth to hers, stealing her words, her breath, both our moans jerking my dick against her thigh. One shift landed me between her legs, and I rubbed the back of my dick all over her pussy, her arousal making a perfect slick path to glide through. Up and over her clit. Grinding. Groaning. Eating at her mouth, breathing her deep into my lungs where she couldn't escape.

Mine.

"Please, Brock," she whispered as I held her lower lip between my teeth and lifted her hips, chasing the tip of my dick. "Please."

I pulled back enough she whimpered, and I released my teeth's hold on her lip. "Look at me."

She blinked, her eyes focusing—and I pressed slowly into her tight heat, jaw clenched to keep from fucking into her like a goddamn animal.

Her lips parted, her pupils dilating as I fed her every damn inch I had to give.

Bottomed out against her womb, my balls flush against her ass, I held still. Gave her time to adjust to being packed full of my dick. She squeezed her inner walls around my girth, and I growled.

"Take it easy on me," I said through grit teeth. "Trying to

be gentle here."

A glint of sass flashed from her eyes, jerking my dick inside her body. "Fuck me, Brock."

"Goddamn you, vixen." I clenched my eyes shut as she squeezed again.

"Please."

With a growl, I let go of my restraint. Let the animal inside me dictate how my body would move, how I would thrust into her wetness, drive her back along my mattress until her head pressed against the wall.

I drank in her cries, soaked in the sight of her tits bouncing with every thrust. Her eyes hazed with passion. Her fingernails ripping at my shoulders. Her heels against my ass urging me to go faster. Deeper.

Fucking harder.

Yanking her leg high over my shoulder, I slammed into her repeatedly, grunting with every thrust, sweat rising to coat my back, my chest.

"Yes," she hissed a whisper, her eyes ensnaring my soul.

I drowned inside her. Her warmth. Couldn't bury deep enough. Couldn't latch onto her soul in the way I wanted.

"Jessie—need. Want…. *Fuck*." I fought to voice what I felt but finding words while her body welcomed my rough taking proved too much.

"More."

So much more—a fucking shit ton.

"Fuck, vixen. Yes." I reached between us, needing to feel her come around my cock, needing her cum to leak down my balls and soak my bed with her scent. Her clit had swelled, and I thrummed my fingertip over the hard nub, sending her lips open to pant.

"Gimme," I managed to whisper past my own need, my balls tightening. "Give. Me."

"Oh, God!" She arched, her pussy clamping down on me like a goddamn vise, and I bit my tongue until I tasted blood to keep from falling over with her. Wetness seeped around my thrusting dick, but still I strummed the hell out of her clit, keeping her thrashing beneath me, her release settling the wild beast inside me.

"Who's fucking you?" I growled, leaning down to bite her lobe, suddenly feeling like I could fuck her all night long.

She gasped, writhing as though needing to get out from beneath me. "T-too much!"

"Who, Jessie?" I bit again, pinching her clit.

"P-please…"

"Who owns this pussy?"

"You," she gasped, still not giving me what I wanted. What I needed.

"Say. My. Name." I growled between thrusts.

Her breath caught, and her second climaxed erupted cum around my dick in a wet rush. "Brock!" she cried out my name, her arms and legs tight as fuck around me.

"Fuck, yes."

My balls fucking detonated, and I dug my toes into my bed, trying to bury deeper—shoot my spunk so damn far up her pussy she'd taste it in the back of her throat. "Shit, baby… Oh, fucking—*fuck*." I grunted and thrust on instinct, hating when my balls emptied, leaving me drained.

Ragged breaths ripped into and from my lungs, and I buried my face in her soft neck, my tongue flicking out to lick the pulse pounding against my lips. "Mine," I whispered the second I could.

Jessie squeezed me tight, and while her lack of vocal agreement didn't sound, I didn't doubt the truth of my words or the clutch of her body holding me tight long after my dick softened inside her.

39

JESSIE

We spent three days eating, sleeping, and fucking. Brock's knee felt well enough by day three he wanted to make the trek back to Shiv's to see if anyone had found the rubble we'd left behind. I talked him into staying put. The less tracks, the better.

He took me to my Beaver's wreckage instead, holding me tight as I cried over her mangled metal.

On day four, he was able to use his solar charger to power up his sat phone and found a handful of texts from his friend Rian. Rather than call and get asked a hundred questions about his silence, he texted back that we both were fine—and that I'd agreed to stay another week.

On day five, I lay sated and sweaty, draped over Brock's chest.

"Will you tell me?" he asked, his lips on my forehead, his fingertips trailing down my spine and shivering my skin.

Neither of us had spoken of what we'd experienced, what we'd felt. While I startled awake at least once a night, I didn't feel as though PTSD would cling to my mind in the years to come. Memories stamped in my head, but I didn't regret what I'd done. The life I'd ended.

Not one fucking bit.

"I read your journal after you left," I said, settling in for a nice long rest on his warm chest. "Read all about the vixen you couldn't keep out of your dreams."

"She's hot as fuck." He squeezed my ass with both hands, rubbing my core against his spent dick.

Light laughter brought a smile to my lips. "You dream in vivid detail."

"Easy to do with the memories I've got locked up inside my head."

My smile faded, knowing more than memories of just me lodged deep in the recesses of his mind—same as me. "Shiv showed up about an hour after you left. He hit me in the head —same place I'd hit when the plane went down."

Brock stilled beneath me, and I let loose with everything I could remember. Every word, every touch, every sensory detail the story brought back to mind, ignoring his curses. He held me close, refusing to give me space when I felt the need to curl in on myself while reliving my whispered conversation with Linny.

"Don't pull away. Please," he whispered. "Let me hold you."

I could stand on my own—didn't need a man—but I gifted Brock what *he* needed. Settling once more, I closed my eyes and listened to his heart thump beneath my ear. Warmth and strength. Protective arms. A heavy sigh left me as I finished with all I could remember, leaving us in the present after whispering about the lack of remorse or guilt when taking Cort's life.

Still, Brock held me.

And I let him.

———

The drone of a plane pulled me upward from stretching out the newly washed sheets on Brock's bed. I grabbed his sweatshirt and hurried outside to find Brock exiting the outhouse, a scowl on his face. We hadn't expected company—but I wasn't surprised to see one of Cort's bush planes circling around to land on the river that hadn't yet frozen over.

Brock met me at the top of the path, and together, we walked down to the river through the snow path he'd shoveled.

"You crashed, and we haven't left the homestead since," he reminded me quietly while waiting along the snow-covered ramp.

The pilot maneuvered close, and we taxied him in. I eyed the man in the passenger seat—Cort's cousin.

"Fuck," I muttered.

"What?"

"Cort's cousin. Sheriff Endsley."

"We know nothing."

"He'll know from cell records that you called Cort after I crashed," I whispered, my insides unsettled.

Brock didn't reply, and we held silent.

Both men hopped from the plane, shoulders hunched against the cold. While the sun peeked over the horizon, it didn't offer much warmth.

The pilot tied up while Cort's cousin approached, lips in a thin line.

"Ms. Blacke."

I nodded, keeping my face blank while wrapping my arms around myself to ward off the chilly air.

"And you must be Brock Charran?"

"Yes, sir." Brock stuck out his hand, and the two men shook without a hint of animosity, thank fuck.

"Sheriff Endsley."

"You here to pick Jessie up?" Brock asked, stepping back to my side.

Cort's cousin glanced between the two of us. "Is that why you put a call through to my cousin close to two weeks ago?"

"Yes, sir." Brock nodded. "He's the only other bush pilot I knew of out here, so I called him the second the weather allowed."

"What happened?"

"I'm sure you saw the wreckage downriver," I muttered, my voice tight as reality sank back in—my plane was gone. Business a bust. Even with cash leftover from Brock's gift, it would take a lot of time and energy to get things going again.

Cort's cousin glanced my way, his eyes cold as always. "And I also see you survived without a scratch."

"Only because of Brock." I barely held back my tears. "Banged up my head pretty bad, though. Was out for a few days."

"Did Cort send you to pick her up?" Brock asked, pulling the conversation back to the reason for his visit—probably to get him the fuck gone.

"He's dead."

I blinked as though surprised, straightening. "What?"

"Dead." His cousin stared me down as Brock offered condolences.

"What happened?" I whispered.

"Not exactly sure." The sheriff glanced between the two of us. "You know Shiv Arntz's place?"

"I used to deliver to him," I said before Brock could reply, my arms holding myself tighter. "Haven't seen him since last summer when I took supplies out to him." I held the sheriff's stare without a twitch. "Why?"

"Cort flew out there a few days ago and thank God he told his secretary where he headed, or we'd still be looking for him. Landed at Shiv's safe and sound, but the cabin burned to the ground. Three bodies inside."

"Oh shit," I whispered, frowning as though upset. "Shiv and his daughter… You think Cort was the third?"

"No tracks leading away from the homestead, so yeah. Autopsy will show if there was any foul play involved."

No tracks—the snow covered them, thank God.

"I'm sorry for your loss, Sheriff."

He stared as though searching for the lie in me, but eventually nodded. "You two been over Shiv's way lately?" he asked, turning to Brock.

"Haven't been off the homestead since Jessie's plane went down," Brock answered. "She only just got out of bed two days ago. Still a bit unsteady on her legs."

"See or hear anything out of the ordinary out here?" The sheriff continued.

"Just an old black bear giving me shit."

Sheriff glanced beyond us toward the cabin. "Once forensics is done over at Shiv's, I'm sure I'll be back."

"Wouldn't know why," Brock said, straightening, "but I got nothing to hide. You're welcome to fly in whenever you want, Sheriff. I'll help in whatever way I can."

Sheriff Endsley eyed him for a few seconds, but Brock didn't blink. Cort's cousin turned his attention on me after a few tense seconds of silence. "You ready to get back to civilization, Ms. Blacke?"

40

BROCK

I tensed for the first time since the sheriff started speaking, my breath held.

Jessie and I hadn't discussed how long she would stay, or what her plans were. We'd been living in peaceful bliss, the days melting into one another as we avoided the sure decision ahead of us.

At least, I had, anyway.

Glancing down, I found Jessie peering up at me, a question in her eyes—quiet as though waiting for me to say something.

What could I say?

I'm falling in love with you.

You belong to me.

Here. With *me.*

That first time fucking after we'd gotten back from Shiv's, I'd flat out staked my claim, calling her mine.

But she'd never agreed. Never answered.

Jessie had weaseled her way into my head, my heart. She'd gotten me to open up and had given me a sense of self-worth I'd been missing. She accepted me, made me feel connected, my life richer.

But she had dreams, and I wasn't going to be the one to hold her back.

"You've got a business to rebuild," I said, my voice gruff, the feeling of a knife in my heart clenching my gut. She was going to leave me—and I was going to let her go.

Jessie blinked as though holding back tears and jerked her head toward the sheriff. "Yeah," she whispered. "I'm ready to leave." Not a crack of emotion in her voice, but no stubborn tilt of her chin, either.

Fifteen minutes later, the plane lifted into the sky, taking my woman away from me, my sweatshirt wrapped around her small frame.

I'd come to the wilderness looking for peace, but the predators of the land had broken me. Jessie had helped put me back together again, and I realized once she was gone, that I'd *found* peace—with her beside me.

And now she's gone.

Jaw clenched against the sting in my eyes and the tightness in my throat, I told myself I'd made the right choice letting her go. Had she asked if I wanted to come with her, though, I realized in that moment, I would have.

I'd found what I searched for in the backwoods of Alaska.

And I gave it up out of love.

41

JESSIE

SIX MONTHS LATER…

He said he would never let me go on that day we ended Cort, but he hadn't fought for me. Hadn't asked me to stay.

That thought haunted my every waking moment, and even though depression wanted to pull me down, keep me in bed every morning, I forced myself to stand. Be strong. Rebuild.

More money had landed in my account exactly two days after I'd left Brock alone, and a painful, stilted conversation over the phone let me know the truth of what I'd expected. He'd sent the money—his gift, one he refused to take back no matter how much I argued.

"You helped me find myself."

One simple sentence had crushed my heart, and I'd bit my tongue to keep from asking why he didn't beg me to stay.

He let me go.

Because he loved me, or because he wanted his silence so he could continue to wallow in his survivor's guilt?

In the few times we'd spoken over the winter months, he didn't mention missing me. Didn't flirt, didn't drop sexual innuendoes or suggestions I fly out for a quickie. He didn't speak of loneliness like the kind plaguing my head and heart.

I wanted him.

Needed him.

I'd gone in, not wanting strings or names, the only way to keep control, but I realized too late, I hadn't been able to hold back my heart. I feared trusting, especially a rich man, but he'd created vulnerable cracks in my walls.

He delved deep.

Claimed me in word.

But not in deed.

I thought it would take keeping my promise to my dad to complete me, give me that sense of belonging I'd lost when my parents had died, but it hadn't. I realized too late that Brock had filled that missing piece in my life.

Too often, I woke in the dead of night, heart pounding, my hands reaching for the warm, hard body I'd dreamed of. I longed for his breath on my neck, the tickle of his whiskers, the wildness in his eyes. I longed for what felt like my other half.

Heartache fucking sucked, but I couldn't find it in myself to blame him. He'd done what he thought was best for me, I felt sure. He just hadn't known *he* was best for me—and I'd never opened my damn mouth to tell him so.

I stared hard at my third cup of coffee, blew out a heavy exhale, and focused on the news I'd heard on the TV the day before.

The tragic events at the Arntz's cabin had been determined to be an accident. It seemed we'd done our job incinerating the place, leaving no trace of evidence to link us to the fire. Even Shiv and Linny's bodies hadn't been able to be identified, just assumed. Cort's dental records confirmed his death.

While it had been found through the autopsies that a knife fight had taken place, no one had been able to ascertain the exact details.

The biggest kick to my gut since leaving Brock?

Cort's cousin had shown up at my front door two weeks after bringing me home, before that information had come to light. My heart had stalled, and blood drained from my face at the prospect of being charged with Cort's murder—but the sheriff had only handed me a manilla envelope, saying I deserved to know the truth of his cousin's hatred.

That truth had brought up my dinner, but nothing could change my love for my father. Not the fact he and Cort, a mere teen at the time, had been lovers, not that he'd invited Cort into my parents' marriage bed. Not the fact the two men had exchanged letters, declaring their love for one another. The last rumpled and stained letter written to Cort had been my father's finally breaking away. Choosing his wife, his daughter, his family, over a jaded lover.

He'd gambled with so much more than money, and even though he'd folded, he lost that bet, too.

By Cort's own mouth, I'd heard of his guilt in causing their accident, but that could never come to light. However, what I'd held in my hands could very well have done the same. Sheriff Endsley offered to reopen the investigation into their crash, but I'd refused.

I let the past lay quiet but struggled to move on physically when what I wanted kept himself hidden away in the wilderness.

Picking back up the list I'd made for Brock's spring delivery, I found my eyes welling, the scribbled words in black ink hazing.

Snickers.

Coke.

Tins of crackers for Chick.

Gummy worms.

The river had still been frozen solid last we spoke, and even though I wasn't scheduled to fly to his homestead until early April, my itch to take to the sky, the longing in my heart and mind drove me to stand.

I'd gotten my father's Beaver back when some of Cort's belongings got auctioned off. Upgraded it with the technology I needed. Gave her a new paint job—and sobbed over seeing Dad's plane all shiny, looking like new, with its Midnight Sun Charter logo in blue on its sides.

I hadn't done all those things on my own—but I couldn't find two fucks to give over the fact Brock had helped. Helping me made him happy, and I wanted him at peace more than I needed to stand on my own two feet.

But I also wanted to see him. Hear his voice, feel his heartbeat beneath my ear. Lose myself in the warmth of his arms, his kiss. Find my fullness in him.

Grabbing up Brock's list, I stood, mind made up.

Time for a trip to Fairbanks, then time to fly.

Hopefully, he'd had enough silence, Hopefully, being without me showed him how much he needed me, too.

BROCK

I loved my wilderness. Loved the snow, the silence of Mother Nature when I stood outdoors, eyes closed, breathing in cold as fuck air, my nostrils stinging. Loved the crackle of the fire, my only companion, when darkness hid the land.

But I loved those brief moments over the phone with Jessie even more.

Three weeks, and I would see her again. Take in her coy smirk, the sassy tilt of her chin, the softness in her eyes I remembered all-too well from our final days together as we'd connected on a deep level I hadn't thought could be broken. Even though distance separated us, I still felt her inside my soul. Could hear her laughter. Remember her sweet scent, the feel of her satin skin beneath my fingertips. The taste of her mouth, the slickness of her body welcoming me inside.

I fucking missed her, missed the comfort of having her beside me, even in silence.

The wilderness hadn't given me the peace I'd longed for —but it had given me a taste of what that felt like before I let her go.

Jessie had been my peace, and I hadn't even realized it until she'd gone, taking my heart with her.

I trudged to the frozen river, my heart heavy and head full. My chest ached from more than the cold air still biting my lungs with every inhale.

The hole in the ice I kept cut and covered with an insulated board to retrieve my daily water, sat a few yards offshore. Nothing stirred, no sound in my ears except the crunch of snow and ice beneath my boots. It would be some time before the ice broke up.

I'd made a mistake in leaving her alone in the cabin, leaving her vulnerable, but I'd made an even bigger one letting her leave me behind.

Trying and failing to push those thoughts aside, I pulled off the water hole cover and quickly filled my two five-gallon buckets.

A low hum jerked my head up. Ears and eyes straining, I stood frozen. Waiting. Heart pounding.

A bush plane appeared like the rising sun on the horizon, stealing my breath. My pulse pounded in my ears, tension flying high to tense every muscle in my body.

Closer.

Louder.

She buzzed overhead, breaking the quiet, the loneliness that had plagued me for countless weeks evaporating at the blue logo on the plane's tail. Midnight Sun Charter. My head tilted backward to keep the plane's belly in sight until my body finally let loose from its seized state, turning to watch as she banked and flew over my cabin.

Jessie.

I grabbed up my buckets and hurried to the shore to get out of her way so she could land.

She'd flown in three weeks early—but I wasn't about to complain.

Wasn't bathed. Didn't give a shit.

Sheets weren't clean. Didn't give a fuck.

All I cared about was seeing her. Breathing her in. Hearing her voice. Connecting, even beyond the physical.

Painted the same as her old Beaver, but skis in place of pontoons, she landed in a kick up of snow on the river.

Jessie hadn't even cut the engine, and I stalked toward the stilled plane, the need to fill my eyes with her like a goddamn tail wind thrusting me forward.

She hopped from the cockpit before I reached her, and I pulled up short, the sight of her petite form all bundled up, winter cap pulled low over her ears stealing my breath. The ultimate high—the best goddamn adrenaline rush I'd ever felt roared through me. The sight of her alone filled me with energy like a live wire, but I waited. Hands fisted. Stare locked on her blue-green eyes. Soaking in the damn *life* she'd brought with her.

A small smile tugged her lips upward, and she shrugged. "Didn't feel like waiting."

I fought to find my voice. Had to clear my damn throat. "I'm glad."

She took a few steps forward, our gazes still locked. "I miss you, Brock."

Couldn't. Fucking. Speak.

A rush of air swelled my lungs as she stopped in front of me, peering up into my face. Sweetness flooded my nose, stiffening my dick.

"Jessie," I choked out her name.

Her coy smirk let me know she knew exactly what she did to me. "I like the beard." She reached up to stroke my cheek, catching my damn breath again. "Wild looks good on you, Mr. Rich Man."

"*You* look good on me, Ms. Vixen."

She shivered, her eyes darkening as her pupils swelled.

"Fucking miss you, too, Jessie," I whispered, my hands finding her waist. "Not letting you go this time."

One of her eyebrows shot up, and she opened her mouth to reply or argue, but I wasn't done.

"When you fly outta here, I'm going with you. Moving into that small house of yours. Adding on a couple additions if you want a bigger place. I don't want them, but if you do, I'll pack the place full of kids, too."

"Kids, huh?" Her chin tilted up, but I caught the glint in her eyes.

"If you want." I tugged her a bit closer until she put her hands on my chest, grabbing hold of my coat lapels. "I know you don't need anyone to make it in this life, I know you're driven enough, strong enough, to do it on your own—but I'm not. I need you, Jessie, and while I've loved living out here, finding myself, I'm tired of going it alone."

She leaned against me, her hands lifting to twine in the curls along my nape. "You're wrong," she whispered, pulling my face down so her breath brushed over my lips. "I do need someone in my life. You told me last time I was here that I was yours. Did you mean it?"

"Never meant that word in a deeper way."

A simple brush of our mouths infused the sweetest ache in my chest, and I pulled Jessie up into my arms, squeezing the goddamn life out of her.

"I want it all," I told her, my voice low, raw—still fucking unsure she'd give me what I needed. "I want those damn strings attached so damn bad I can't breathe."

"How's that mattress holding up?" She nipped at my

lower lip, and I groaned, my dick aching and leaking to stuff her full.

"Empty."

"Want to go fill it up?"

I grabbed hold of her ass, and she wound her legs around my waist. "Not letting you go, Vixen."

"Good." She buried her cold nose in my neck and let out a heavy sigh I'd ached to hear again. "I'll stay here with you if it's what you need, Brock."

Pausing on the path halfway to the cabin, I pulled back my head to look her in the eye. "You're the life I've been searching for. You're my peace in the wilderness. The breath in my lungs, and the beat in my heart. I want you to stand on your own two feet—but you better fucking believe I'll be right beside you. Doesn't matter where. Holding your hand. Holding you up if that's what you need."

She pressed her lips to mine. "Just need you."

"You have me. Always. Fucking forever."

I made short work of the rest of the path, kicked in my cabin door, and laid my woman out on my lonely bed. "I'm gonna blow like a goddamn teen the second your wet heat clamps around my dick," I warned her, yanking off my coat, filling my eyes up with her body wiggling to rid itself of clothes. "Been too fucking long."

"You won't leave me hanging," she said with assurance, her husky voice breathless to the point I had to grip the base of my dick and squeeze to keep from shooting off.

"Damn right, I won't."

"Brock," she whispered my name, gaze latched on mine, her fingers trailing down between her thighs as her legs lay open.

"Yeah, Ms. Vixen?" I zoned in on the wet pink she rubbed against, my mouth salivating, dick dripping.

"I want strings attached this time."

Fuck, yes. I tore my attention up from her teasing fingers. "How about names?"

A coy smirk lifted her lips. "Meaning *last* names?" She knew exactly what the fuck I meant.

I kicked off my last pant leg and climbed up onto our bed, our so much damn emotion radiating from her eyes my heart ached at being so full. "If you'll have me."

"Jessie Charran…" Her eyes twinkled as she reached for me. "I like the sound of that."

I groaned in complete fucking agreement, settled between her thighs, and slid the back of my dick up through her soaked folds. "Hold on tight," I warned her, notching inside her body. "Gonna fuck you so damn hard you'll feel me in the back of your throat."

"Fuck, yes."

Thrusting filled me with a sense of home I'd never understood before. Hadn't ever hoped to find.

"Mine," I groaned into her mouth as her pussy clamped down on my length.

"Damn right."

Her whisper hit me right in the goddamn chest, and I focused on showing exactly who she belonged to, not stopping until we both collapsed in a tangle of sticky, sweaty flesh—at complete peace.

THE END

———

———

ABOUT THE AUTHOR

Lynn Burke is an international bestselling and award-winning author. A stay-at-home mom, she's a lover of coffee and vino, and with three spawn and two fur babies underfoot, noise levels dictate the daily switch-over time. In her few quiet 'me' moments, she can be found hunched over her Mac, trying to type as fast as her muse spews hot stories.

You can find more about Lynn at her website: www.authorlynnburke.com

ALSO BY LYNN BURKE

Abel's Obsession

Divulging Secrets

Healing Storms

In Between

Reluctant Lumberjack

Resisting his Mate

The Playboy Bachelor

Billion Dollar Love Anthology

Blood Born Series

Bonds of Worship Series

Dark Leopards MC

Darkest Desires Series

Devil's Outlaws MC

Elite Escort Series

Fallen Gliders MC

Forbidden Obsession Duet

Found by Fate Series

Midnight Sun Series

Missing Link Series

Risso Family Series

Sandy Ridge Series

Vicious Vipers MC